Killer Bear For Hire

AXEL HATCHETT MYSTERY VOL. 5

Steven LeRoy Nelson

BLOOD AND THUNDER PRESS

BLOOD AND THUNDER PRESS
3612 Sheffield Lane
Colorado Springs, CO 80907
www.bloodandthunderpress.com

ISBN: 194046904X
ISBN-13: 978-1940469041

To my little root beer barrel.

1

I never thought much about bears until I met the Hatfield brothers. They weren't related to the Hatfields who had that little misunderstanding with the McCoy family, but there were similarities.

Ambrose and Cuthbert lived out in the hills like old-time Colorado mountain men, in a log house with damned little electricity and no plumbing to speak of. They'd both been married and spoke bitterly of their ex-wives at every opportunity. But when Ambrose, the elder of the two, visited my private investigator's office in Quartz Quarry, he didn't want to talk to me about the former Mrs. Hatfield. He talked about a bear.

"It might be a grizzly," said Ambrose. He was a big guy with a face battered by the wind, the sun, and a few fists. "There's still a few here in Colorado. Or it could be a very big black bear. I'd guess it weighs a good four-hundred pounds. It's got a hump on its back like a grizzly, but the face is all wrong. Cuthbert and me think it might be a cross-breed."

"Half grizzly, half black bear?" I asked. "I didn't know there were such things. I didn't know they dated."

"They're rare, but it happens sometimes. The offspring are mostly barren, like a mule." He looked at the fancy new nameplate on my desk. It says, Axel Hatchett, Private Investigator. "Say, how'd you end up with a name like Axe, or, Axel? Your folks in the lumber business?"

"No, but they always spoke highly of Lizzie Borden. You say this bear is trying to kill you and your brother?"

"No question about it. It already nibbled on Cuthbert's leg a little. I doctored him. It was chasing him and he climbed a tree, thinking he was dealing with a grizzly."

"Grizzlies don't climb trees?"

"No, sir. I never heard of a case. But this bear climbed right up after my brother. Cuthbert had a rifle slung over his shoulder — he'd been chased by the bear before and just made it back to the house — but by the time he got his rifle unslung and in shooting position, that bear dropped from the tree and took off.

"Smart, that's what that bear is. And me, well, I've had some experience with that bruin myself. One day I was just coming out of the privy and that old bear was waiting for me. I chucked a big rock at him and high-tailed it to the cabin. It was a close call. We've been dealing with this particular varmint for two months now. It's getting to be aggravating."

"Why isn't this bear hibernating? It's March."

"That old idea about bears always holing up in winter just ain't so. If they can still get food, sometimes they'll stay awake all winter."

"I see. I'd never heard that. Listen, have you called the cops, or the forest rangers, or whoever?"

"Sure. The cops tried shooting it, but with handguns, like that's going to work! The forest service fellow tracked the bear, but then the tracks just disappeared. He couldn't find it, no how. We called the dog catcher, but he wouldn't do nothing about it. Scared, he was. We even called our local sheriff, but he's close to 80, and he scarcely gets out of his rocking chair."

"Can't say as I blame either of them."

"Maybe not. Well, then we tried hunting it ourselves, but we could never get a good enough look at it to shoot it. We hired a professional hunter, a guide. He couldn't find that bear at all."

"How can a thing that size just disappear?"

"Makes you wonder, don't it? But me and my brother have an idea about that. We think that bear is trained. It's somebody's bad pet."

"A pet? Who'd keep such a thing?"

"You've heard of trained bears, I reckon. We think somebody's taught that bear to go after me and Cuthbert."

"For what purpose?"

"Don't know. Could be me and my brother have rubbed a few folks the wrong way over the years."

He shifted in his chair. His gray hair — he must have been around forty — was greased down and, he was sweating. Donned in a worn corduroy suit and a string tie, he was all gussied up for his town visit. When he shifted in his chair, his coat fell open and I saw the handle of a big hunting knife worn on a fancy tooled belt.

I don't think he trusted town folks much. He was a tough-looking guy. I think he would have been happier living in the 1850s rather than the 1950s.

"Would anybody get anything out of you should you and your brother meet with an untimely demise?"

"You mean if we got killed? Sure. Our boys would get all our money and property. We've made our wills. I've got two sons, and Cuthbert has two himself. They're good enough boys. They just come out of the wrong women's nethers, but they can't help that. Maybe one of the ex-wives wants us dead. They both act like it. Also, me and Cuthbert own a good piece of mountain land. Our Granddaddy bought up enough land to start his own state.

"When we decided we'd had as much as we could stand of town living, and dealing with our ex-wives, we sold off a good part of the land. But we kept the best for ourselves. We also kept

Granddaddy's old log house and fixed it up.

"The truth of it is, we're surrounded by land you could use for timber, or grazing, or building mountain homes on. We've even got our own spring — plenty of water. The mineral rights might be worth something, too; I'd guess there's some gold on our land. Not to mention there's a nice lake. Some might want to kill us so that our land could go up for sale.

"Like I was telling you, our boys will inherit everything, exceptin' they're minors still. The moms would get control of the land and money until our sons were grown."

"OK — so somebody wants you dead. Why use a bear for a weapon? What's wrong with a gun, or poison?"

"I think they're making sport of us. They're having fun getting us killed." He leaned forward in his chair, putting his face close to mine. He smelled of whiskey and something else, maybe beef jerky. "I'll tell you this, whoever's doing this to us is going to end up as dead as that old bear is going to be. I don't know what your Bible says, but mine tells me that vengeance is mine."

"My Bible doesn't say that. It says something about vengeance belonging to the Lord and nobody else. Maybe you've got a bum copy. Did you snag it from a motel room?"

Ambrose's face was as dark as leather, but he flushed almost purple. I'd made the mountain man mad, but that was all right. I like stirring up my clients. Sometimes they tell me things they wouldn't otherwise.

"Don't go speaking lightly of the Good Book."

"Sure. Mind backing up a bit? You're after-shave's not to my liking."

"Aftershave? I got a beard."

"I noticed. Tell me, who hates you the most?"

"Harvey Rundell, I expect," He leaned back in his chair. "Because of the lake." He coughed into his fist. "I don't suppose you'd have a drop of whiskey in that desk of yours? I could use a nip. I've always heard you detectives keep a bottle handy."

"Not me. Sorry. I guess I'm not much of a detective."

"That's all right. I've just been working up a thirst doing all this talking. Me and Cuthbert live private, and we ain't much for palavering."

"Mr. Hatfield, what is it exactly that you want me to do for you?"

"Sure, let's get right to the point. Cuthbert and me were thinking you could come out to our place and look around a little. You could talk to folks, figure out who might want to train up a bear to kill us. That's in your line, ain't it?"

"Talking to people? Yeah. I might be able to help you. How far out in the mountains do you live?"

"Out by Flinders Cone, about thirty miles from here. The roads aren't much. Do you have a truck, or an old Jeep?"

"No. Maybe I could borrow one."

"Sure. Or me and Cuthbert could take you around in our truck. We don't have a whole lot to do. Hunting, fishing, trapping, keeping the old cabin roof from leaking. Stuffing birds."

"Stuffing birds?"

"It's a hobby. We've got stuffed birds all over the house. Magpies, crows, blue jays, even a couple of eagles. It helps pass the time."

"I see. I guess you could loan me that truck of yours."

"No, sir. Begging your pardon, but nobody's allowed to drive the old Jimmie but me and my brother."

"It's better if you don't have to drive me around. Your presence might make people less cooperative. I'll see if I can borrow a truck."

"Or buy one. I've heard you detective fellows are pretty well off."

"You're making me feel bad. I don't keep a whiskey bottle in my desk drawer, and I'm not rolling in dough. Anything else you've heard about detectives that I ought to know?"

"Well, I've heard you're crack shots with those little sawed-off revolvers you carry. And I guess you're pretty free with the ladies. They just fall into your laps, so I'm told."

"The only one who falls into my lap is my wife." I pointed to a big picture on my desk of Tracy, all fixed up in a wedding dress and smiling like a loon. I was pretty proud of that picture.

"Oh, you married? I feel sorry for a man who's hitched. Marriage sure didn't work for me or my brother. How can you stand living with a woman?"

"I'm a newlywed, and I couldn't be happier. Maybe some of us gents are better cut out for marriage than you and your brother."

"I expect so." He moved around in my rickety client's chair and it creaked and complained. He was a heavy guy. "When do you think you'll be coming out to see me and Cuthbert?" He scratched his gray-streaked brown beard, looking for ticks.

"I'll need to draw up a contract. Fortunately, for you, I'm not working on any other cases right now. I'll have to look around for a vehicle I can borrow. How's tomorrow or the next day sound?"

"That'll work fine. We'll try to keep alive that long."

Mr. Hatfield and I agreed to terms and I pecked out a contract on my old Remington. He paid me a generous retainer from a roll of well-thumbed bills he pulled from a pants pocket, then he drew an elaborate map on the back of an envelope that showed me exactly how to get to the Hatfield estate. I shook his meaty paw and the deal was done.

"Do you have a telephone at your place?" I asked.

"We do. We use it mostly for talking to our sons." He wrote the number on the envelope he'd drawn the map on. "Pleasure doing business with you, Mr. Hatchett."

"I'll do everything I can to help you, Mr. Hatfield."

He clumped out of my office and got into his Jimmie truck. I smiled.

I was working again. I felt relieved. I looked around my swell new office. It didn't even have any cobwebs or dead bugs in it yet, and it smelled only mildly of the cheap cigars I smoke.

Tracy and I had gotten married on New Year's Day, and now it was already March and I'd scarcely worked a day during those two months. That's not the way a new husband is supposed to behave, but there was nothing I could do about it. I'd already sold my Nash Airflyte, which still left us with Tracy's old brown Chevy. I'd even helped out in the sandwich shop where Tracy worked. It was owned by our landlords, Ben and Allie Ozhammer. So, getting an honest-to-God investigating job was a relief.

However, I needed the loan of a truck or a Jeep. I went next door to the sandwich shop. My office and our apartment are in the same building. Tracy was behind the gleaming counter selling a small-headed guy in coveralls a baloney and cheese sandwich. The place smelled like cold cuts, fresh-baked bread, and various condiments. It was the kind of smell that makes a guy hungry.

Ben and Allie were working too, though it was mid-morning and not very busy. They were a middle-aged couple, both shaped like squat bowling pins, and they always had goofy grins on their faces. They were the happiest people I'd ever met. I don't know what was wrong with them. I smiled at Tracy and gave her a thumbs up.

"I'm working again," I said. "See, your husband's not such a bum."

"Great! Is it going to be an interesting case, my little Tootsie Roll?"

"It involves a trained killer that's a bear. What do you think, my little root beer barrel?"

"Right down your alley."

"Yes, Tracy?" asked Allie, thinking she'd heard her name. "You want something?"

"Just talking to Axe," Tracy said.

I buttonholed Ben. "Listen, Ben, I've got a favor to ask. And if the answer's no I'll understand."

"A favor?" His smile got even bigger. I wondered if all people from Romania were as jolly as him. "For you, of course. Whatever you want."

"I'm going to be spending some time out in the boonies. I'm on a case."

"I knew you'd get work, a fine detective like you. It sounds like a so interesting case."

"I was wondering if I could borrow your truck for a few days. I'll be traveling on rough roads, and I know that truck of yours is your baby, so if you don't want me driving it on rotten roads, just say so."

Ben rubbed at a spot of ketchup on his long apron. "You'll be careful. I know you will. You're a great driver, being a detective. All those fast car chases."

"Sure." So, I was supposed to be a lady-killer, a crack shot, an ace driver, and loaded with dough. It's swell being a detective. "I'll need it tomorrow."

"That is fine. Tracy can loan us her Chevy. Is that all right?"

"Of course it is. Listen, I really appreciate this."

"Not a worry. There's gas in the truck and everything."

"I'll fill it back up before I return it to you."

"As you wish. Good luck with this so interesting bear investigation."

"That reminds me. I don't suppose you'd have a bear gun I could borrow, do you?"

"A gun for a bear? No. All I have is the old forty-five we keep under the counter, for the thieves. We've never been robbed, me and Allie, but it pays to be careful."

"That forty-five's bigger than anything I've got, except for my twelve-gauge. I want something I can carry on me."

"Of course. Take the gun. It is like they used in the old West."

"It's still the old West. I'll trade you my thirty-eight until the job's finished."

"This is good. Are you staying in the mountains for this case of yours?"

"Maybe. The place I'm going to is a good thirty miles from town, and the roads, I'm told, are bad."

"You have to leave your Tracy, for days? So sad for newlyweds."

"I agree, but the job comes first. We need the money."

"Of course. Give our Tracy a big kiss before you leave."

"Don't worry about that."

I went and gave my counter girl a peck on the lips and journeyed back the ten steps to my office.

My new bride really was sad the next morning. So was her new husband. Tracy's brown eyes were shiny and a couple of tears spilled out of them.

"Don't be like that," I said. "I'm not going off to the swamps of South America. Flinders Cone is only about thirty miles from here."

"I worry about the bear."

"You better worry about him." I played with my hat, letting our two kittens bat at it. "That bear doesn't have a chance against old dead-eye Axe Hatchett."

"Promise you'll be careful."

"I'll swear my oath on a box of King Edward cigars."

"Swear on whatever you like," she said. "Just don't let that mutt bear get you."

"Listen, I may not even be staying up there. I don't know what kind of accommodations the Hatfield's have for me. I tried calling them, but they didn't answer their damned phone. I'll try again."

I did just that and got ahold of Cuthbert. I told him who I was and asked whether or not I'd be staying in the mountains while I did my investigating.

"You can. We got a little cabin behind our own. It ain't much, but it will keep the snow off you."

"That'll work. Say, the bear can't get into that little cabin, can it?"

"Not unless he learns how to turn a doorknob, which I wouldn't put past him. You got a gun?"

"An old Colt forty-five, and a double-barreled shotgun."

"Keep them close. When do you think you'll be here?"

"Soon as I can. I'm starting right now."

"See you then. You got a truck?"

"I do. I'll see you when I get there."

I packed a suitcase and gave Tracy a goodbye kiss. She was crying. So was I, almost. My bride's perfect nose was pink, and she hadn't combed her wavy reddish-brown hair.

"I wish I could go with you," she said.

"You and me both. Maybe next time."

Tracy and I had just stepped out our front door when Ben came out of the sandwich shop.

"I know you are getting ready to go on your interesting investigation," Ben said to me. "But Allie is home with our sick boy. He can't go to school, with his fever so high. We are busy."

"I'll be right there, Ben," said Tracy.

"Yes, but could you, Axe, come in and help a

little? We are so busy. There must be a storm coming. People are always hungry before a storm."

"Sure, I'm in no hurry," I said. "I'll be happy to come in and help."

2

Even with three of us in the sandwich shop, it was crazy busy — hungry mouths everywhere. I didn't take off my apron and my funny hat until well after two. Oh well, Tracy and I could use the money. I called the Hatfields again and explained that something had come up and I'd be out to their place later than I'd hoped.

Right before I left, a guy walked in who I thought I'd never see again — Cookie, Tracy's old boss. He owned Rocko's Kitchen, where the grease is always hot and free. He'd come to beg Tracy to come back to work for him. He was practically crying.

"Tracy, you got to come back. We're losing business without you," Cookie told my bride. He had a voice like a congested bulldozer.

"Sell the place," said Tracy, with a nasty edge to her voice I hadn't heard for a while. "What's your problem? You've got Prissy May."

"She's too nice, not like you. The customers

walk all over her."

"Too bad they aren't walking all over you. You could use some shoe prints on your face, then you'd look like your mother. I'm staying here. I like this shop. The customer's behave like actual people, and my new bosses are really good to me."

Ben and Allie stood a few feet away with worried looks on their round faces.

"I'll give you a raise. I'll give you a second day off every week," Cookie said. "I'll give you a share of the profits."

Tracy snorted. "What profits? Listen, Cookie, there's nothing you can offer me that will make me leave Ben and Allie. They're like angels. Cherubs maybe."

Cookie waved his hairy hands around and pulled off his hat and threw it on the floor. "You gotta come back."

Ben stepped forward. "Excuse me," he said to Cookie, "this is a nice place. Folks come here for a quiet meal. People do not throw hats on the floor and shout and wave hands around in Ben and Allie's. Please go. I can make you a sandwich to go with you."

"You couldn't make me eat one of your lousy sandwiches," said Cookie, and he stormed out of the place.

"Good riddance," said Tracy.

Allie came over and put her plump arm around Tracy's shoulder. "I'm so glad you don't go with him. We'd miss you too much. And that man's a pig. Excuse my so bad language."

"I wouldn't think of leaving you and Ben," said Tracy.

She rubbed tears from her eyes and smeared some jelly on one cheek at the same time. It looked kind of cute. I kissed the jam off — it was strawberry — and made my exit. I climbed into Ben's truck and headed for Flinders Cone.

About twenty miles outside of Quartz Quarry, the roads turned bad. Then they got worse — little more than dirt wagon tracks. Ben's truck was an old 1937 Studebaker Express. In spite of its 19 years, it ran swell, and I drove slow. I soon entered a heavily-wooded area; there were dense stands of pine, and fir, and spruce, and groves of aspen. After a few more miles I passed a thinner stand of trees and got a glimpse of a lake. That meant I was getting close to the Hatfield's place.

I turned onto a path — you couldn't call it a road — and after a mile I came in sight of a big log cabin with a green roof. There was a Jimmy GMC truck parked in front of it. A couple of big dogs, mongrels splashed with multi-colored spots, came around the side of the house to greet me with their sharp barks, but their tails were wagging.

I'd scarcely parked the maroon Studebaker before the cabin door opened and two men stepped out onto the wide porch. Cuthbert was as big as his brother but not as gray. Both men had the same features, but while Ambrose wore the cautious look he'd had in my office, Cuthbert's face was split into a big, dopey, grin. His face, like his brother's, had been beat up by rough weather and some hard fists. He wore a walrus mustache and thick spectacles.

"Welcome," he said, stepping off the porch to shake my hand. "Don't mind the dogs. Spotty and Doc don't have no harm in them."

"Don't you worry about the bear getting them?"

"No. They've learned their lesson. They keep away from that bear."

I noticed that Cuthbert was walking with a slight limp.

"I hope you've learned your lesson," I said, nodding at his leg.

"I'll be glad when that varmint's dead, that's for sure."

I grabbed my suitcase and my shotgun from the truck and followed the brothers around the side of the house. There was a much smaller cabin there, and it wasn't much to look at. The log walls still had the bark on, and the roof was as sway-backed as Humpty Dumpty's saddle pony.

"You'll have to share our outhouse," Ambrose told me. "But your little cabin has a good wood stove and its own pump in the little kitchen. There's an old pie safe on the porch you can keep eggs and bacon and milk in. It'll keep them cold."

"Or you can just eat my cooking, if you want," said Cuthbert.

"I've eaten worse," allowed Ambrose.

I wished I'd brought such supplies. I was getting hungry and Cuthbert's cooking didn't sound that promising.

"We've got some stew simmering over the fire," Cuthbert told me. "I'm the cook around here. Hope you like squirrel."

I'd never tasted that particular rodent, but I didn't tell the brothers that.

"Squirrel. My favorite," I said. "Is there gravy?"

"There is. And some wild onions, and a few roots I dug up in better weather."

Speaking of weather, it could have been better. There was snow on the ground, of course, but none in the air. However, it was cold and windy. I was happy to step into my little home-away-from-home. The brothers showed me around.

There was a screened-in porch on the front of the cabin that was harboring some junk and the promised pie safe. Inside, the cabin was one long room with two tiny windows, one on each long side, with strips of flannel blanket for curtains. The brothers had been kind enough to build a fire in the stove that stood in the middle of the one-room cabin.

The room contained an iron bedstead with a quilt, a lumpy-looking mattress, and a flattened pillow. There were some shelves on the walls, a small table with an oil lamp — unlit — and a primitive-looking rocking chair. The kitchen area had a cupboard for a pantry, a long counter, and a sink with a pump handle sticking out above it.

"Looks very homey," I said.

Cuthbert grinned like he'd built the place himself. Maybe he had. Ambrose told me to take my time getting settled, and then to come over to the big house for an early supper.

"Thanks," I said, and the two men left me to myself.

I left my suitcase unpacked and kept my overcoat on. I had the forty-five Ben had loaned me in my right coat pocket, and it felt like it weighed about thirty pounds. It didn't fit in my pocket very well. It had a seven-and-a-half-inch barrel and looked like the kind of gun Wyatt Earp would have cottoned to.

I went out onto the porch and out the door — I wanted to look around the place. Both cabins sat in the middle of a clearing full of ancient stumps and some saplings. The logs to build the cabins had obviously been harvested right here, creating what was now a large open space. I trudged through the snow, circling the clearing, looking for bear tracks. Actually, I had no idea what bear tracks would look like, but I figured they'd be big. Spotty and Doc showed up and followed me around.

On all sides, there was nothing to see but trees, rocks, and patches of cold sky. I saw some tracks in the snow that might have been made by rabbits, or squirrels, and that reminded me of the supper that would soon be on the table. I lit up a cigar and paced around some more then headed for the big house.

When I knocked on the door, Cuthbert let me in and the dogs trailed in after me. Cuthbert was smoking a corncob pipe. I guess there was tobacco in it, but it smelled like a butcher's dirty socks.

Ambrose was sitting at a big wooden table in the substantial living room, sewing up the belly of a bird he'd stuffed. It was an owl. It looked a bit lopsided, and its glass eyes were crooked. In fact, there was a frightening array of deformed-looking birds perched on the long shelves that lined the log walls. They stared at me with their beady glass eyes. I tried not to return their stares.

"I think this owl might be my masterpiece," Ambrose told me, with pride in his voice.

"It's certainly life-like," I lied. Actually, it couldn't have looked more dead if it'd been flopped in the road with a coyote gnawing on it.

"Supper's still simmering, but it's almost done," said Cuthbert. He wore a stained apron. "There's sourdough biscuits and a prune pie. There's also plenty of coffee, and there's whiskey to go in it."

"My mouth is watering," I said.

"Let's talk about the bear," said Ambrose, getting right to the point. He propped the deformed owl in the middle of the table like a ghoulish centerpiece.

I grabbed a wooden kitchen chair, pulled it over to the table, and sat down.

"I've already told you the bear's big," said Ambrose. His big furry face was a bit red and I suspected he'd been hitting the moonshine "And smart. But I haven't told you how single-minded he is when he's trying to tear the vitals out of me and Cuthbert. He's determined.

"He's left the dogs pretty much alone since he attacked them the one time. Doesn't seem interested in bothering nobody but me and my brother. Our sis, Bethany, has been out to visit us several times, and has even stayed the night. She's never seen that bear! Our sons have been out here, too. The bear ignores them. It don't pay attention to strangers, neither."

"That bear," said Cuthbert, as he stirred the contents of a large iron pot that was hanging over the fire in the big stone fireplace, "has got Ambrose and me in his sights, and in his head. He might as well have blinkers on when it comes to anybody else."

"And you told the cops all this?"

"Yes," said Cuthbert. "They don't believe us. They didn't say so, but that's how it is."

"What about the forest service guys? Did they listen to you?"

"Some, but they kind of looked at us sideways, too," said Ambrose.

"Do you two carry guns when you're out wandering around?"

"We hardly step out of the house without our rifles," said Cuthbert. He was wearing dungarees over long johns and sported a fine brace of red suspenders "But that bear — we call him the Reaper — "

"As in 'Grim'?"

"That's right. The Reaper, he's a sneaky one. I half expect him to drop down on one of us from the roof, or a tree, or a big rock. Every day, me and Ambrose get more gray in our hair."

"Maybe you should move."

"No, sir. We're staying right here. This place was built by Granddaddy. We used to come visit him and Granny when we were kids. We lived in town, but we always liked coming out here. Granddaddy taught us to hunt, fish, trap, and track. Lots of good memories."

"And we ain't going to get scared off our own place," said Ambrose, with finality.

"Better that than to be buried here," I said.

"But you're going to fix all that," Ambrose told me. "You're going to find out who owns the Reaper, and you're going to bring him to justice."

"That's my plan," I said. "Who do I start with — that neighbor you told me about?"

"Harvey Rundell?"

"Yeah. Why does he hate you two? What's your lake got to do with it?"

"Well," said Ambrose, "we don't let him fish in our lake no more. And Harvey lives to fish. There's not another lake like ours around here. It's full of trout because only me and Cuthbert fish in it. We used to let Harvey fish there, too, just to be neighborly."

"We made him give us half the fish he caught," put in Cuthbert.

"But Harvey got on our bad side. He started inviting other folks to fish in our lake. Some sand he's got."

"So we set the dogs on him, though they wouldn't have hurt him. He hates us for that. But if we won't let him fish in our lake anymore, it's his own fault."

"Sis is coming out here tomorrow," Ambrose told me, "Our baby sister, Bethany — I told you about her. You might want to talk to her, see if she knows more about who might hate her brothers than we know."

"I'll be happy to talk to her."

"I got to warn you, though. She's our sister, and we don't want you laying your hands on her."

"I told you I was married."

"She's a looker," said Cuthbert. "You might not be able to resist."

"I'll keep my eyes shut when I talk to her. How's that?"

"Just keep your distance," said Ambrose. "Sis is a lot younger than us. And she could be in pictures if she wanted to."

"I'll keep that in mind," I said. I couldn't imagine any sister of these two lantern-jawed, clown-nosed, hicks belonging in anything but a monster movie.

"Supper's ready," said Cuthbert.

Ambrose moved his owl and taxidermy para-phernalia off the table, and Cuthbert set it with crockery plates — chipped and faded — bent forks, tarnished spoons, and dull knives. He set out big mugs of strong coffee, carried over the stew pot, then fished a Dutch oven out of the coals and put it on the table. It was full of good-smelling biscuits. We dug in.

To my surprise and relief, the squirrel stew was tasty. It wasn't tough like I'd feared, and no more gamey than some cheeseburgers I've eaten. The sourdough biscuits were perfect, and when we got to the prune pie I was startled by its actual edibil-ity. The butter for the biscuits had come out of a mold and was better than butter generally is.

"You guys have your own milk cow?" I asked.

"Two," said Cuthbert. "In the barn."

"I didn't see a barn when I was looking around," I said.

"It's in the woods a ways. The cows sleep there. And we've got some chickens. The barn locks up tight. We don't want a fox or a coyote helping themselves to a chicken dinner."

"Or a bear helping himself to beef," said Am-brose.

"Seems like you're pretty well fixed out here," I said.

"We are," said Cuthbert. "We got a hutch of bunnies in the barn, too, for when it's not hunting season. We eat a lot of rabbit and squirrel, and trout."

"Deer and elk, in season," said Ambrose.

"How do you keep the meat from going bad? An elk's a big animal."

"We got our own smokehouse," said Ambrose.

"We don't go hungry," said Cuthbert, shoveling half a buttered biscuit dipped in gravy into his craw. "We even put in a garden in summer, though most things don't grow worth a damn. Still, we get some carrots and squash and such."

"We live like kings," said Ambrose, belching loudly. "Pardon my French."

"It's my second favorite language," I said.

After we'd eaten, I helped the boys wash up. There was no indoor plumbing so we used water heated over the fire.

"When it gets good and dark," said Ambrose, "we'll head outside and see if we can scare up that bear for you."

"Much obliged," I said.

3

We killed some time until dark talking about bears and other matters. I watched the brothers play a couple of games of checkers — Ambrose cheated, and Cuthbert let him — and then it was dark enough to go bear hunting. Ambrose grabbed up an old thirty-ought-six rifle that was leaning against the wall, and we headed out the door. It was damned cold and the wind had picked up.

"We'll show you the barn while we're out here," Cuthbert told me. "You'll have fresh eggs for breakfast. And smoked bacon. We raised a hog last year."

They led me out into the woods until I was good and scared. Finally, in the light cast from a big moon in a clear night sky, I saw the bulk of an old log barn.

"We won't go inside," said Ambrose.

They kept taking me deeper and deeper into the forest. There were night noises. Not pleasant ones.

Some predator was killing a squeaking rabbit, and I could have sworn I heard the chuff of a bear.

"That's not him," said Cuthbert. "Reaper don't make any noise usually, unless he's attacking. Even when he was chewing on my leg, he was silent as the grave."

"It was almost your grave," I pointed out.

We'd walked what seemed a mile, saying little, our footsteps crunching in the snow underfoot. I thought I saw something moving in the trees not too far from us. Then it started moving faster. Whatever it was, it was charging us.

"Look out!" shouted Cuthbert.

Ambrose had the rifle to his shoulder in a second. The thing in the trees let out a growl loud enough to scare a timid detective. Then suddenly the beast was on us: a bear as big as Ben's truck. It roared, and so did Ambrose's rifle. The bear kept coming. It ran into our midst and started striking out with its big front paws. We found trees to climb, and we climbed them. I pulled my feet up as far as I could. I'd polished my shoes only three days earlier and I didn't want the bear slobbering on them.

Halfway up a swaying pine, Ambrose jacked another round into the chamber and took what aim he could in the moonlight, but before he could fire, the bear was suddenly gone. It just took off and disappeared into the dark woods.

"Stay where you are for a piece," Ambrose told us. "He might be circling around to come at us from behind. I'm sure I hit him."

We stayed in our trees for another ten minutes, maybe longer. I was in favor of staying on my perch all night.

"I think he's really gone," said Ambrose. "Maybe he's dead."

Ambrose scrambled down out of his pine tree, scattering needles onto the snow. Cuthbert and I climbed down as well, chipping bark off with our heels. Yours truly was the last on the ground. I thought I smelled fear. It was coming from me.

"Let's look for his blood spoor," said Ambrose.

We must have spent twenty minutes looking for blood — Ambrose had brought along a flashlight — but it was too dark under the trees to see well. We found plenty of bear tracks, and our own tracks, but not a trace of blood anywhere.

"I don't see how I could have missed him," Ambrose complained.

"The light was bad," said Cuthbert. "Nobody could have made that shot."

"I could have. I did."

"Maybe it's a ghost bear," I volunteered.

"Don't be a fool," said Ambrose. "Let's get back to the house."

We trudged our way back to the big cabin. The fire glow from the fireplace showed through the windows and looked very comforting. We went inside, stomped the snow off our shoes, and huddled in front of the fire for a time. Then Cuthbert lit a couple of oil lamps and asked if anyone wanted more pie.

"No, but I'll take more coffee," I said.

We all drank coffee. The brothers poured generous doses of whiskey into theirs. Cuthbert lit up his smelly corncob. Ambrose rolled and smoked a cigarette. I didn't have a cigar on me, but I wished I had.

"I thought you said that bear didn't make any noise," I complained. "It sounded like a giant meat grinder."

"I said he only makes a noise when he's attacking," said Cuthbert. "And that was sure enough an attack."

"I know I shot him," Ambrose muttered.

"Then where's the blood?" asked Cuthbert.

"I don't know. It don't make sense." Then, to my surprise, he said: "It's time for bed. We turn in early out here, Mr. Hatchett. Breakfast's at six."

"Six? OK"

Cuthbert offered to take the rifle and a lamp and escort me to my own cabin, but I was feeling too much like a coward to act like one.

"I'll be all right," I said, bravely. "It's only twenty yards from here." I pulled the Colt hog leg from my coat pocket and got a good grip on it. "Good night, gentlemen. See you at breakfast."

Trembling with fear and cold, I hurried my way to the one-room log hut. I closed the door behind me, latched it, and resisted the urge to dive under the quilt on the bed. Instead, I lit the oil lamp, then loaded some wood into the stove from the stack I found against one wall. I also found a couple of old army blankets to add to the quilt.

I smoked a cigar, the smoke blending with my frosty breath, until the cabin warmed up a little. Then I took off my shoes and climbed into bed. If there'd been shutters on the windows, I would have closed and latched them. I left the lamp burning, as a night light, and peered out from under the covers to watch the flickering shadows on the wall. It took a good long time for me to fall asleep.

Twice during the long night I woke up thinking I'd heard growling and chuffing outside my cabin. The lamp had exhausted its oil and had gone out. In the darkness, I waited for the sound of splintering wood or broken glass to announce the entrance of my bruin friend, but nothing happened.

I kept Ben's thumb buster under my pillow and tried to go back to sleep. I'd set the old windup alarm clock I'd brought with me for five-thirty, and damned if I didn't fall back asleep about five minutes before it went off.

I'd brought a flashlight along with me in my suitcase, in case of need, and I used it when I walked to the big house for breakfast.

"Sleep well?" Cuthbert asked, as he opened the door for me.

"Sure, like a hibernating bear. And you?"

"No. Ambrose snored too much. Our rooms are right next door to each other. Coffee?"

"Please. Hot and strong."

Cuthbert expertly crafted a breakfast of fried eggs, bacon, and perfectly-formed flap jacks. I ate my fill. Nothing like a fearful night to set up a man's appetite.

"You fellows been up long?" I asked.

"Since four," said Cuthbert. "I had cows to milk, rabbits to feed, and eggs to gather."

"You weren't afraid old Reaper would catch you in the dark?"

"I had my rifle. Still, I haven't breathed a quiet breath since that bear started stalking us."

"I can imagine."

"As soon as it gets good and light," said Ambrose, who had hardly spoken to either of us, "I'm going out to look for Reaper's blood. Anybody going with me?"

"I will," I said, though it was the last thing I wanted to do.

"I wish you'd forget about that blood," said Cuthbert. "I'm telling you, your aim wasn't as good as you thought."

"I couldn't miss a shot like that. I got him. Maybe we'll find his carcass. I surely do look forward to hanging his pelt above the fireplace."

"You and me both," said Cuthbert.

"Here, here!" I said, and I meant it.

"Bethany will be out later in the morning," said Ambrose. "I'd sure like to show her that dead bear."

"He just won't give up," Cuthbert whispered to me. "That bear ain't killed."

"Quit whispering," demanded Ambrose. "I know what you're saying, and you're wrong."

All three of us went out into the woods to look for blood spoor. We didn't find any, once again, but we found lots of footprints. Ours and the bear's. The crazy beast had circled around us a couple of times while we were in our trees, and then had headed for the high country.

Finally, Ambrose found a pine tree with a broken branch down low. It was between where Ambrose had been when he'd fired and where the bear had been.

"That's what happened," Ambrose crowed. "My bullet hit that branch and was deflected."

"That branch could have been broken by anything," said Cuthbert.

"Don't argue with me," Ambrose said.

We trudged back to the cabin.

"Tell me more about this Rundell guy," I said.

"He's a card," said Cuthbert.

"He's a crazy fool," said Ambrose. "Nobody likes him. He's all the time causing trouble. He doesn't have many neighbors, but he's rubbed them all the wrong way. You know what he likes to do? There's a wire fence all around his property. He owns about a hundred acres. He goes out in the woods and moves his fence posts a little farther out onto other folks land. He's trying to change the boundaries without anybody knowing it. It's a trick he's been up to for years. He gets caught at it, and then he has to move the fence back where it belongs. But he never gives up. And what does he get out of it? Nothing."

"Does he have a temper?" I asked.

"Like a volcano," said Cuthbert. "You don't want to get him mad, but it's hard not to. After he invited all those folks to fish in our lake, and we set the dogs on him, he came over and wanted to shoot poor Spotty and Doc. We put a stop to that. Boy, was he mad. Turned as red as a lobster."

"Cursed us, too," said Ambrose. "A blue streak. I got pretty riled myself."

"When did you forbid him the use of your lake? How long ago?"

"Oh, about a year ago," said Cuthbert.

Ambrose nodded. "Long enough time for him to train up Reaper and set him on us."

"Does he have any background in working with animals, training them?"

"Not that I know of," said Ambrose. "Nobody knows much about Harvey. When he's not mad, he's a closed-mouthed man. Might have worked for the circus for all I know."

"I'll want to talk to him. Where's he live?"

"You know the road that runs by the lake? The one you drove up on yesterday? His property's on the other side of that road, right across from the lake."

"So your land ends at the road?"

"Yes, damn it," said Ambrose. "Granddaddy bought up a whole lot of land, including where the lake is, but the land Harvey lives on was already bought up. All along the road there, for miles. We don't like having neighbors so close. Cuthbert and me has thought of building a new house, farther out in the woods."

"It don't seem right, though," said Cuthbert. "Granddaddy built this log house himself, and it don't seem right to abandon it."

"We'll stick where we are," said Ambrose.

I still had my overcoat on: it was cold. Unfortunately, the big gun in my pocket kept trying to fall out. That long barrel didn't make it much of a pocket pistol. The brothers noticed me fussing with it, trying to make it fit my pocket better.

"You know how to shoot that thing?" Ambrose asked me.

"I haven't shot this particular revolver, no. But I'm not a bad shot."

"You got shells?" Cuthbert asked.

"Yes." Ben had given me a box of fifty rounds.

"Let's do some target practicing."

There were some heavy-duty metal trash cans in back of the big house. They had special lids on them that could be fastened down to keep scavengers out. Cuthbert dug around in one of them and collected a bunch of tin cans. While he was setting them up on a big stump I went into the little house and fetched my cartridges.

We stood about fifty feet from the stump. Cuthbert had set up six cans in a row.

"I'll take the one on the far left," I told them.

I cocked the hammer, took careful aim, and

squeezed off a shot.

Boom! The can flew up in the air and clattered down in the snow. I felt pretty proud.

"Let me try," said Ambrose.

I handed him the gun. Without even appearing to aim, he shot three times. Boom! Boom! Boom! The next three cans in the row jumped up in the air. The first one hadn't landed before the other two were in the air.

"Straight shooting," I said, a little envious.

"My turn," said Cuthbert.

He took the gun and backed off another twenty-five feet. He aimed and fired off two quick shots. The last two cans flipped off the stump.

"Wild Bill Hickok and Doc Holliday," I said. "Remind me not to make you fellows mad."

They both laughed and gave me my gun back. I reloaded it.

I wanted to head over to Harvey Rundell's place and have a chat with him, but I decided to wait until I'd talked to Bethany, who Ambrose said would be out in a little bit.

"Your sister married?" I asked the sure shots.

"We told you to leave her be," warned Ambrose.

"Is she or isn't she?" It graveled me to think these old coots thought I was trying to make time with their baby sister.

"She's a widow," said Cuthbert. "She's got a couple of little girls, as sweet as can be."

"What does she do for a living?"

"Teaches at the grade school some, as a substitute. But she don't really need to. When we sold part of Granddaddy's land, Bethany got a third of the money. And her husband left her some money, too. We're all pretty well set up when it comes to money."

"Not that we're rich or anything," said Ambrose.

"But we aren't hurting, and neither is Bethany," said Cuthbert.

I sat around with the brothers in their living room, and we drank coffee, smoked, and talked about all the different bears they'd seen — and sometimes shot — while we waited for Bethany to show up. Around ten o'clock, a blue Dodge pickup, a few years old, pulled up the drive and parked in the open spot in front of the cabin. A woman got out. She was short, with a lot of dark hair pulled back in a ponytail. The fur-collared coat she wore hugged her full figure.

We all went out to greet her. Close up she looked about thirty or thirty-five. She was carefully made up, but I expect she would have been beautiful even with her face scrubbed. She had a kind of Ava Gardner look to her, and her voice was husky and low. Her smile dazzled like sun-lit snow.

"This here is our baby sister, Bethany," said Ambrose. "Sis, this here is Axe Hatchett, a detective. I told you about him on the phone yesterday."

"A pleasure," said Bethany, extending a small gloved hand.

"The pleasure's mine," I said, shaking the little paw. Ambrose gave me a dirty look.

"Axe here would like to palaver with you a little," said Cuthbert. "He wants to know your slant on this bear business."

"I don't know much about it," purred Bethany, "except that it's terrible. I don't want anything happening to my brothers."

"Come in and have a cup of coffee and we'll talk," said Cuthbert.

"I'm about coffee'd out," she said. "And I'm stiff from sitting in that truck. I wouldn't mind a walk."

"Sure, we can walk," said Ambrose.

"I'm sure you boys have better things to do. Perhaps Mr. Hatchett will take me for a stroll."

"Call me Axe," I said.

Ambrose glared at me. "Suit yourself, Sis. We'll be inside when you come back. By the way, Axe, have you talked to your wife lately?"

"I'll give her a call when I get back," I said.

4

Bethany slipped her small arm through mine and we walked slowly away from the house. It wasn't as cold as yesterday, and the sun had even managed to find a hole in the clouds to shine through. We headed out toward the lake.

"Do you want to see the lake up close?" she asked.

"Sure, but I'm not much for ice fishing."

Her laugh was like an audible string of pearls.

"You'll have to excuse my brothers. They've always been protective of me. I don't think they've ever accepted the fact that I'm all grown up with children of my own."

"Tell me about the bear."

"I only know what Ambrose and Cuthbert have told me. I'd rather talk about them."

"OK. Give me your best gossip."

The laugh again. "They're good brothers, good men, but a little rough around the edges."

"I've been called that."

"I doubt if you've made as many enemies as they've made. The Hatfields have a reputation for being hard to deal with. There's a toughness to us that grates on some people's nerves."

"Surely you're not like that."

"Me? You don't know me. I'm a Hatfield, right down to the marrow. But I'm not like my brothers. They were always tough, but the war did something to them. They both joined the Navy as soon as the war broke out in '41. I don't know what kind of action they saw. They've never talked about it much, but they both came home with souvenir Japanese skulls."

"That's pretty grizzly."

"Yes. Our parents were killed in a car accident while Ambrose and Cuthbert were still away in the war. They took it pretty hard. So did I. They found girls to marry, and had kids — nice strong boys. But the marriages didn't have a chance. I don't know...maybe my brothers spent too much time with men in the Navy. It's like they forgot how to behave around women. I'm afraid they were rather rough with their wives."

"You mean they beat them?"

"Yes. Ambrose beat Kelly. I don't know if Cuthbert actually beat Melinda, but both of their marriages ended, and it was the wives who ended them. Since then, Ambrose and Cuthbert have grown more and more anti-social. They live like hermits. If it wasn't for their sons, and me, I don't think they'd have anything to do with people.

They both used to work construction jobs in Quartz Quarry, but after their divorces they sold off a bunch of land and basically retired."

"Did the ex-wives get any of that money?"

"Some, though there was a long legal battle. My brothers hung onto as much of the money as they could. And their wills leave everything to their sons. They love their boys, and they see them two or three times a week when it works out."

"Are these ex-wives bitter?"

"No doubt. But would either of them sic a trained bear on my brothers? I can't see it."

"Who would?"

"Harvey Rundell's crazy enough to do such a thing. However, my brothers have plenty of other enemies. They don't treat their neighbors well. It's surprising that they ever let Harvey fish in their lake."

"Would any of the other neighbors want the Hatfield brothers dead?"

"Probably. The kind of people who choose to live out here, Mr. Hatchett, can be pretty ornery. Eccentric. Even dangerous. They don't necessarily pay much attention to the law. They're like vigilantes."

"The Hatfields and the McCoys?"

She laughed again, giving me a shiver down my spine. "Thank God there's no one named McCoy around here!"

We had reached the lake. Snow covered the ice, and there were animal tracks on it. A cold breeze swept along the frozen lake and chilled us.

"Let's go back," she said.

"If you want. Thanks for talking to me."

"If you need any more information, or help, call me. I'll give you my number."

"Thanks. Listen, it's none of my business, but as a newlywed I've developed a greater interest in people's marriages than I used to have. You're a widow. How did your husband die?"

"Have my brothers been talking to you about me?"

"Only a little."

"I made a big mistake. I married a man who was a lot like my brothers, and like our father. After we'd had our kids — two beautiful, delightful, girls — I wanted out of the marriage. Ralph beat me. I don't even like to admit that, but it happened."

"And then he passed on."

She stopped and looked me in the eye. Her eyes were a miracle of blue flecked with green. "I killed him. I shot him with his own gun. I got off on a self-defense plea."

"Oh." I was a little shocked. "I guess you really are a Hatfield right down to the marrow."

"At least I didn't keep Ralph's skull."

She laughed again, but there was an icy edge to it this time.

"I've got another question, if you don't mind. I've noticed that you talk a little more — educated — than your brothers. They're strictly backwoods boys. How'd you turn out so different?"

"I was always a big reader growing up. And early on I decided I wanted to be a teacher. I won a scholarship to go to Flinders College."

"I see. That explains your more hifalutin speech."

When we reached the house we went inside and started another round of coffee drinking. The brothers were very solicitous of their sister. They helped her into a chair, brought her coffee, lit her cigarette, and guarded her from me. If they hadn't treated their wives well, it wasn't because they'd forgotten how to behave around women, like Bethany had suggested.

When I was warmed up again I asked for more specific directions to Harvey Rundell's place, then headed out in Ben's pickup. I said good-bye to Bethany before I left.

"I may not be back before you leave," I told her. "Thanks for the talk."

"My pleasure. Oh, let me write down my phone number for you."

Both Ambrose and Cuthbert bristled up like porcupines.

"Did he ask for your number?" Ambrose asked Bethany, rising from his chair.

"No. I offered to give it to him. He might need information about the bear." She smiled teasingly, "Your dear friend, Reaper."

A little past the lake, on the opposite side of the dirt road, was a rural mailbox on a post with the name "Rundell" sloppily painted on it in red. There was also a gate across the drive, and a cattle guard. I wondered if it was to keep the cows in or out. The gate was closed but not locked. I opened it and drove about a quarter of a mile until I reached a brown house with a red roof.

I parked the Studebaker out front and waited. Country folks like to have a little time before they receive visitors. Unfortunately, this particular country boy obviously didn't want visitors at all. The front door immediately opened and a dog charged out to my truck, barking like it was rabid and was thoroughly enjoying its condition. It was a big, mangy, ugly mutt, just a little smaller than a bread truck.

I waited some more. When nothing happened, I got impatient. I figured that whoever had loosed the dog on me was watching from a window. I hauled the revolver out of my overcoat pocket and rolled down the driver's door window, and then stuck the gun out and waved it around a little. That got action. A man came rushing out the front door. Fortunately, he wasn't toting a shotgun. He strode into the middle of his yard and yelled at me.

"What do you want, mister?"

"Call your dog off. This is the second time this morning I've had dogs sicced on me. What's wrong with you folks? Was Santa bad to you this Christmas?"

The guy walked out to the truck while he

shouted at the dog to shut up. The dog looked at him, then at me, and kept on barking.

"I said shut up, Larky!"

Larky quit his barking and backed away a little.

"This here's private property, mister."

"Your gate wasn't locked. I came over here to talk to you about your neighbors, but it looks like you're just as unfriendly as they are."

"Which neighbors?"

"I don't know. The ones who own the lake. I guess."

"The Hatfields." He made a disgusted noise and spat in the snow. "They ain't friendly, no. Were you ice fishing?"

"Trying to."

He looked suspiciously into the bed of my truck. "Where's your gear and tackle?"

"I left it at the lake. Their damned dogs didn't give me a chance to grab it. And now I come over here and there's another damned dog. I'll shoot him if I have to. And if you get in the way, I'll shoot you, too." I waved the gun around some more. I figured I'd throw a temper fit. If Harvey Rundell was known for going off like a hand grenade, I'd go off like a mortar. We could have a contest. When we both got tired, maybe we could get down to talking regular.

"Don't wave that gun around, and don't threaten my Larky."

I got out of the truck. Larky stayed where he was. Harvey Rundell pulled a forty-five automatic out of the pocket of his red plaid winter coat and pointed it at me.

"Mexican standoff," I said.

We glared at each other. Harvey was a big guy, though short. He looked about sixty, but it's hard to tell with these mountain dwellers. They get a lot more sun and wind on their pretty complexions than the rest of us. I've seen country-bred teenagers that looked like Grandma Moses.

"Put your heater up and I'll put mine up, too" I said.

We both slowly returned our weapons to our pockets.

"So, the Hatfield's sicced their dogs on you, did they? Just for trying to do a little fishing. That's Ambrose and Cuthbert for you. No hospitality in them at all. Want to come in for some coffee?"

"Sure." So that's how he was going to play it. He was going to provide an example of how people in these parts are supposed to behave. Fine with me.

We went inside the house. It was smaller than the Hatfield abode, and newer. It was a bit cluttered, but I gathered that Harvey was a bachelor. He had an honest-to-God electric stove in the kitchen, with a blue-speckled coffee pot on one burner. He poured us each a cup and we sat down. He fished a pint bottle of hooch from a canister that was meant to hold flour.

"Snort in your coffee?"

"No, I've already had a little too much. You

know how it is when you're ice fishing. A bottle doesn't last long."

"That's sure the truth." He poured a generous shot of whiskey into his coffee and stirred it with a thick red finger. "I used to fish in that lake all the time. Why not? There's enough trout in there for the whole county. But when I invited a couple of my friends to join me one day, the Hatfield's sent their damned dogs after us. They haven't let me dip a line in that lake since. And that's a damned shame, because I love to fish."

"Who doesn't? Too bad you can't get rid of those Hatfields. Maybe they'll sell their place to someone friendlier."

"No. They'll be there until they die."

"That so? Then let's hope they die soon. When I cut my hole in the ice, I could see trout all over. It's like that lake is carpeted with them."

"Don't tell me. I like to fish, and I like to eat fish."

"There ought to be a law," I said, vaguely. That's always a good line to get people talking.

Larky pushed his way into the kitchen through a dog door, took one look at us, and went back outside.

"I sure hope that bear gets those two Hatfields. Serve them right", said Harvey.

"Bear?" I asked innocently. "Is there a marauding bear around here?"

Harvey burst out laughing, then shook his head. He topped off our coffee, then poured another snort of hooch into his.

"I heard it from Lester Flarks, just down the road. Lester's a queer old duck. His wife, too, and they've got some queer ducks for kids. I don't know where Lester heard about the bear. Story is, there's some kind of bear, maybe a black, might even be a grizzly, though I haven't heard of a grizzly in these parts for years. That's fine with me. You ever see a grizzly bear?"

"In the zoo."

"You ought to see one in the wild. That'll make your hair stand on end. But this bear Lester was telling me about, it's a big one, kind of brown-and-blond. It's been stalking the Hatfields. It don't seem to bother nobody else."

"That seems a bit odd, don't you think?"

"Yes, it does. Only thing I can figure is those Hatfield's must have shot at it or something when that bear was just a cub. It remembers and is out for revenge."

"Do bears do that kind of thing? Are they that smart?"

"Smart as whips. I wouldn't put anything past a bear."

"I don't know. Sounds almost like somebody's trained the thing if it's going after two specific people. Is that possible?"

"You've heard tell of dancing bears, haven't you?"

"Sure, but that's a little different from training a bear to kill somebody. I don't know. I don't have any experience training animals. Do you?"

"Trained German Shepherds when I was in the Army. I've broke horses. And I've taught Larky all kinds of tricks. Want I should call him in and show you?"

"That's all right. Maybe this Lester Flark is just pulling your leg. You said he was a queer duck."

"Yeah, but he ain't a liar. Doesn't have enough imagination. That's a bear with a chip on its shoulder. It wants to kill Ambrose and Cuthbert, and that's a certainty. Couldn't happen too soon, if you ask me."

"This Flark, he lives up the road? Does he share your dislike of the Hatfields?"

"Oh, yeah. Most everybody does. Folks around here have been shot at by the Hatfields. Had their trucks beat up with baseball bats. Had their women folk mashed on."

"You don't say?"

"It's mostly Ambrose. Cuthbert's got some good in him. When Larky got caught in a coon trap last fall, it was Cuthbert that brought him back to me. He'd already bandaged up the dog. Told me not to ever tell Ambrose he'd done me a kindness. That's how it is."

"Thanks for telling me all this. I just came over to see if you knew who owned that lake That bear story interests me. Think this Lester Flark would talk to me?"

"You got another bottle in that truck of yours?"

"I do."

"Lester will talk to you as long as that bottle lasts."

"Would he be home today?"

"Likely. He does a little construction work in the summers, but he mostly does nothing when it's winter."

I stood up. "Thanks for the coffee, and the conversation," I stuck out my hand. "My name's Cyrus B. Comstock. Freelance butcher."

Harvey stood up, shook my hand. "Harvey Rundell. I do a little of this and a little of that. Good to meet you."

Rundell escorted me to my truck, maybe to keep Larky from becoming too sportive with me. We shook hands again and I drove off. He hadn't seemed as unfriendly as the Hatfield's had indicated. Maybe they weren't very good judges of character.

5

Before we'd parted as chums, Harvey had told me exactly how to get to the Flark residence. I drove back past the lake, went on two miles further, turned right down a road that looked more like a dry stream bed, and kept going until I came to a big house painted cow-pie green. There was an old Dodge Power Wagon, Army surplus, parked in the front yard. No dogs were in sight.

After a minute I got out and went up onto a porch whose roof looked like it was about to collapse. I knocked on the door and a man wearing a dirty undershirt and dungarees answered the door. Heat from an overloaded woodstove poured out the doorway like dragon's breath.

"Yeah?" He didn't seem overly friendly.

I'd told Harvey the truth. I did have a bottle in my truck; a pint of pretty decent whiskey. I don't keep any in my office because I'm not interested in lubricating clients, but I keep a bottle with me when I'm out talking to anybody who might help me with a case. Whiskey is a good icebreaker. I had the bottle in my overcoat pocket now — the pocket opposite where I kept the gun. I shivered as I brought out the bottle and broke the seal.

"This cold just gets right down into my bones," I said. I took a very short snort, then offered it to the guy I hoped was Lester Flark. His eyes lit up.

"Thank you kindly, don't mind if I do." He poured a couple of ounces of the saddle varnish down his throat, his big Adam's apple jumping up and down. "What can I do for you? Lost?"

"Hope not. Looking for a Lester Flark."

"You found him. Come on in." He kept the bottle in his hand.

He led me to a worn couch with sprung springs and grandly waved me to be seated. He sat in an old rocker with a calico seat cushion and back, much nearer to a wood stove that roared like a locomotive and glowed an eerie orange.

"Know what you mean about the cold getting into your vitals. Thank God for cord wood and whiskey." He took another generous gulp from my bottle and handed it back to me. "What's you here for? Don't get many visitors except for them's that's lost."

"My names' Devlin Lockworthy. I'm employed by the Tarpin and Hankshaw Two-Ring Circus. Heard of us?"

"Think so. Think I took the kids to that circus one year."

I looked around. There were no kids, but I

guessed they were in school.

He seemed to read my mind. "Kids are in school today. Much good it will do 'em. Wife's at work. Dogs are chasing a coon. Looks like it's just you and me."

"I'm looking for a runaway bear, Mr. Flark."

"Call me Lester. A bear? Dangerous?"

"I hope not, but he's got a mind of his own. He got away from us when we were down in Utah. Nearly killed a child and its mother, though they're both OK now. I've been tracking him ever since. I heard about a bear that was seen in this area that matches his description. I've been talking to folks.

"A Mr. Harvey Rundell said you might know something about our wayward bruin. It's a big bear, about four-hundred pounds, kind of brownish-gold, with a humped-up back and sort of a sneer on its face. Does that match the description of the bear you were telling Mr. Rundell about?"

"Well, I guess it does, from what I've heard. But, to tell the truth, I ain't actually seen that bear. Only heard tell of it. It's been pestering the Hatfield brothers. Come close to killing one of them, I heard."

"They haven't been whistling at it, have they? Because Cassias — that's the bear's name — can't abide whistling. We always warn the crowds and the hot dog venders."

"I can't say if they whistled at him. Maybe so. It might make sense, because that bear don't pester nobody but the Hatfield boys. I don't know them well. I don't know if they're whistlers."

"I'll tell you what I'm afraid of, Lester. Cassias — according to my information — has been in this area for some time. Maybe two or three months. It doesn't make sense. He's a fugitive. You'd think he'd keep on running. I'm wondering if somebody around here has kind of taken to Cassias. He does have a lovable side. Could be they've turned him into some kind of pet. I was wondering if you happen to know if there are any ex-animal trainers around these parts. Could you name any?"

Lester thought about it. He thought so long that I finally handed him the bottle again. He took a slug, but didn't hand the bottle back.

"Let's see. You talked to Harvey. He trained dogs in the war to kill Nazis."

"I don't think Mr. Rundell has our bear."

"Probably not. I'm just trying to think of something. Hop!"

"Hop?"

"Hop Carlson. They call him Hop on account of one of his legs is shorter than the other. War wound. He kind of hops when he walks, though he dances just fine. Me and the missus, we went to an Elks Club dance one night last spring, and Hop and his wife — she's tubercular — they were dancing like it was doomsday. He —"

"Mr. Flark?"

"Yeah?"

"Does Hop have a background as an animal

trainer?"

"Hell, yes. I was just telling you." He took an-other pull from my bottle. "He told me once that he worked for some damned zoo in the swamps of Florida. No, it was Louisiana. Some little mom and pop zoo where they trained the animals to do tricks. They had alligators, a tiger, monkeys, a damned hippo, and — by God! — a bear. Hop trained them all. He lost just the very end of one finger once. I think it was the gator that done that."

"Does Hop live around here?"

"Sure he does. No more than two miles from here."

"Could you give me directions?"

"I can. But he won't be home this time of day. He drives a delivery truck down in Quartz Quar-ry. He works until five, I believe. Me and the mis-sus, we're tight with the Carlsons. Now why couldn't I remember about him being an animal trainer?"

"Just slipped your mind, I imagine. Do you have the Carlsons' phone number?"

"Probably got it written done on the pad by the phone in the kitchen. Let me go look."

Lester left the room. I noticed he wasn't wear-ing socks. He came back in a minute.

"Here it is. I wrote it down for you." He handed me a dirty scrap of paper with a number scrawled on it in pencil.

"Thanks," I said. "Could I use your phone?"

"Sure. It's in the kitchen. Oleander hasn't cleaned up in there yet. She works, you know. Excuse the mess. I expect Effie, Hop's wife, will be home. She can't work because of the tuberculosis."

I followed Lester to the kitchen and cleared away a stack of dirty dishes to unencumber the phone. I dialed the number. It rang five times.

"Hello?"

"Is this Mrs. Carlson?"

"It is. Who is this? Not the plumber?"

"No, ma'am, I'm not a plumber. I work for the circus. I was wondering if I could speak with your husband."

"He's at work."

"All right. What time does he get home?"

"Around six. Could you call back? I'm getting ready to go out. I was waiting for the plumber to call, but that's not going to happen."

"Sorry to bother you. Could I drop by this evening? I want to talk to your husband about his days with the zoo in Louisiana."

"Are you offering him a job?"

"No, ma'am. I'm looking for a runaway bear."

"I haven't seen any bears. But you can drop by if you want. But no earlier than seven and no later than nine. I guess my husband might be able to help you."

"Thanks so much. I'll probably see you around seven."

"You know how to get to our place?"

"I'll get directions from Flark."

"Oh, are you at the Flarks? Tell Lester hello."

"I will, ma'am. Thanks."

I hung up. I went back in the living room and Lester was tippling from my bottle again. I let him keep it.

"How do I get to the Carlson's place?"

He drew me a map. Another damned map.

I drove over to Hop and Effie Carlson's house. The drive entailed a good many twists and turns, even if it was only two miles from the Flarks'. I even lost my way once. I finally found the place, a rambling concrete-block house painted lime green. I hoped no one would be home. There were no cars in sight.

I went up on the porch and rang a door bell. No one answered. I tried again. Still no answer. I pounded on the door with my fist. No reaction. Not even a dog barking. I walked around the house and tried to look in the windows. There was nothing much to see. Furniture, appliances. No people or dogs.

Good. The house was built in a big clearing in the woods. I walked around the grounds. There was a horse trailer that looked suitable for ferrying bears. I looked inside it. It had been swept clean. I could scarcely find any horsehair, and I wouldn't have known what bear hair looked like.

There was a small barn in the backyard, but the big doors were locked up. There was also a window, but I couldn't see anything but horse stalls and a small tractor. I checked out another outbuilding, also locked — it was big enough for a bear to sleep in — and there was a storage shed of some kind beside it.

I looked all over the ground for tracks. I found some dog tracks, but where was the dog? Maybe Effie had taken it with her wherever she'd gone. I didn't find any bear footprints, but I still had hopes that Hop Carlson was the man I was seeking. I wondered what he had against the Hatfield brothers, or if he was working for somebody else.

It was almost two o'clock. I was hungry. Tracy had packed a couple of sandwiches for me when I'd been working in Ben and Allie's. They were in the glove box, so I ate them. I couldn't think of what to do. I decided to head back to the Hatfield place and pick their brains a little. I wanted to know what they thought of Hop, and what crimes they might have committed against him.

I also wanted to know about their former wives. So far, all I knew was their names. It would be a good idea to talk to both of the ex-wives. They could be suspects. One of them might have hired Hop, or someone, to set loose the Reaper on Ambrose and Cuthbert. Even Bethany was a suspect, though it broke my heart to think so. She'd shot her husband, maybe in cold blood. If she felt less tenderly about her brothers than she claimed, she might want to help them into their graves for some reason.

The case was clearly screwy. Whoever heard of someone using a bear as a murder weapon? I got back in Ben's truck and headed for the Hatfield cabin.

Ambrose and Cuthbert were still at home, playing checkers. A couple of exciting guys. Bethany had gone back to town. When I walked in the door, my nostrils were pleasantly assaulted by the smells of Cuthbert's cooking.

"What's for dinner?" I asked.

"We're having venison stew for supper. Hope you don't mind stew two days in a row," said Cuthbert.

"Not your stew. It smells great."

"Any luck with your detecting?" Ambrose asked.

I shed my coat, found a chair, and lit up a cigar.

"Oh, I talked to two or three people. I'm going out again this evening to visit Hop Carlson." I waited to see what reactions that name would get. Neither man moved or said anything. Their faces remained impassive.

"Hop Carlson," Ambrose finally volunteered. "What's he got to do with this bear business?"

"I don't know yet. Maybe nothing. But he used to train wild animals at a zoo down south."

"That right?" asked Cuthbert, pricking up his ears. "Say, I didn't know that."

"What's he got against you guys?"

"I guess he might not be too happy about his horse," said Ambrose.

"It was an accident," said Cuthbert.

"Exactly what kind of accident?" I asked, pricking up my own ears. I could feel them flapping back and forth on my head.

"Shot one of his horses," said Cuthbert. "The horse was on our land, maybe a mile from the house here."

"So you shot it for trespassing?"

"Hell, no," said Ambrose, angrily. "We aren't that kind of folks. Cuthbert was deer hunting. He'd tracked a deer for a good hour and it was starting to get dark. He thought he spotted it in a stand of aspen. He shot it. Only it wasn't a deer. It was one of Hop's horses. He keeps two of them, rides them some, but mostly rents them out to a dude ranch in the summers. One of them got out of Hop's pasture. Probably jumped the fence."

"And wandered way over to your place?"

"It's only a few miles. Anyway, Hop wasn't too happy about it. He wanted us to buy him another horse, or pay him what it was worth."

"You mean you didn't?"

"That horse was on our property without our permission. Cuthbert didn't mean to kill it."

"Yeah. Still, it seems the decent thing to have done was to pay him for the horse. You guys act like you've got the money."

"Are you saying we aren't decent?" Ambrose challenged me.

"All I'm saying is that if it'd been me, I would have paid for the horse. That's just me. Maybe I'm an idiot."

"You can do whatever you want with your

money, Hatchett. I'll spend mine the way I see fit. Hop should have kept his horse in his own pasture."

"He's got another now, anyway," said Cuthbert.

"Does he have anything else against you?" I asked.

"Not that I know of," said Ambrose. "Maybe he didn't like the way we treated him. He got good and mad at us about the horse. I got tired of listening to him. Finally up and popped him on the jaw."

"The guy's got one leg shorter than the other. Did you ever hear about fighting fair?"

"You don't seem to care much for us, Mr. Hatchett," said Ambrose.

"I don't have to care for you. I'm trying to track down that bear we met up with last night. I need to figure out who owns it, if 'own' is the right word. As long as you pay me my money I don't have to like you."

"Ambrose is in a bad mood," Cuthbert told me. "Don't mind him. I beat him five times in a row at checkers today. And he's none too happy about Bethany going off with you and telling you God knows what secrets about the Hatfield family."

"She didn't tell me any secrets. She told me you two have enemies, maybe for good reason, but she didn't give any details. She said she killed her husband. Self-defense. That's about all she told me."

"Ralph deserved what he got," said Ambrose. "I'd have killed him myself if Sis hadn't."

"He was a skunk," said Cuthbert.

"Worse than a skunk."

"Listen, guys, how do I go about getting cleaned up around here? I mean, do you have a shower, or a bathtub?"

"We got a bathtub," said Cuthbert. "You're welcome to use it. I'll have to heat up water for you."

"You don't have any electricity at all? No hot water heater? No plumbing?"

"It suits us," said Cuthbert. "We've got a Delco generator. It gives us enough electricity to run our fridge and a big freezer. What meat we don't smoke goes into the freezer."

"What you can do," said Ambrose, "if you don't want to wait for hot water, is you can go over to your place. There's a pump. Have yourself a sponge bath. Come back at supper time."

I wasn't feeling altogether welcome. I went over to the little cabin, pumped some water into a big kettle, heated it on the stove, and luxuriated in the sponge bath Ambrose had recommended. Then I laid down for a nap. Fear of the Reaper had disturbed my sleep quite a bit the night before. That, and the cold. I actually slept for a couple of hours, then changed my clothes and headed over to the big house. I was looking forward to the venison stew.

"Supper's almost ready," Cuthbert greeted me.

"You play checkers, Mr. Hatchet?" Ambrose asked me.

"Call me Axe. I've played a game or two."

"I'm getting tired of playing with Cuthbert. I think he cheats."

You're the one who cheats, I thought.

"I'll play a couple of games with you," I said. "After we've eaten, of course."

"Stew's ready," said Cuthbert. "There's more biscuits. And I made up a pie with some canned peaches."

"Sounds swell," I said.

6

Ambrose was surprisingly nice to me that evening. He didn't even cheat at checkers or complain when I beat him. And when I brought up the subject of his ex-wife, he was willing to talk about her.

"It all started out fine," he told me. We had put the checker board away and were quietly digesting Cuthbert's excellent venison stew and peach pie. I was drinking more coffee, and the brothers were each having a big whiskey and water. "Kelly was as sweet as honey in your mouth when we met. But that all changed after we got married. You know how women are. I know you just got hitched, but you'll soon find out what a woman's really like once she starts wearing your ring.

"It was after the kids came that she really changed. She thought she knew more about how boys should be raised than I did. She didn't want me touching them with my belt. Hell, Daddy's belt did me nothing but good. Kelly wanted to bring my fine sons up as sissies. I couldn't put up with that! I put my foot down, and she couldn't handle it. Always was willful. Cuthbert didn't have any better luck with his mate."

"That's a fact," said Cuthbert.

It was six-thirty and I needed to head over to the Carlson's.

"You need directions?" asked Ambrose.

"No. Lester Flark gave me directions."

"You've been all over the county already, haven't you?"

"Just asking folks questions. There's a lot of leg work and mouth work in my job."

I remembered I hadn't talked to Tracy since I'd said good bye to her. That was unforgivable. I borrowed the Hatfield's phone and gave her a ring.

"Hello?"

"Is this the wife of Axe Hatchett?"

"The proud wife of Axe Hatchett. Is this the husband of Tracy Hatchett?"

"The proud husband of Tracy Hatchett. Listen, I'm sorry I didn't call sooner. You know how it is."

"How's the case going?"

"Maybe pretty good. I'm not sure yet. Did our bed seem a little empty last night? I know my bed here felt awfully lonely."

"Our bed felt about the size of Texas. Come back as soon as you can, but don't hurry on my account. I know you've got work to do. Can you tell me anything about the case, and the bear?"

"The bear and I had a fateful meeting last night. The Hatfield brothers and I ended up climbing trees."

"Oh, no! Are you all right?"

"I still have all my limbs. So does the tree I climbed. And I had Ben's revolver with me. I'll be OK. I've got to go now. I wish I could talk longer, but I've got to drive over to an animal trainer's house."

"Lucky you. Be careful, my little boiled snail. Sleep well tonight, but not too well. Call me when you can."

We made kissy noises at each other and said good-bye. When I hung up both brothers were looking at me funny.

"Newlyweds," said Cuthbert, rolling his eyes.

"He'll get over it," said Ambrose.

I climbed into my coat, checked my bear gun to make sure it wasn't falling out of my pocket, and headed for the Studebaker. I drove the long and tortuous route back to the Carlson house. There was a three-quarter-ton truck in the drive, and an old Jeep next to it. I hastened to the porch and rang the bell. The door opened.

"Are you the circus man?" a plump, loud-voiced woman asked me. If this was Effie, she sure didn't look or sound tubercular. Maybe Lester had gotten his diseases mixed up.

"He couldn't make it," I said. "I'm a detective. I'm working with the circus man." For the life of me I couldn't remember what name I'd used. "I'm Axe Hatchett. Is Mr. Carlson in?"

"Just watching TV. Come on in."

She led me to a sort of den. Hop was polite enough to get up and turn off the television. He walked with a noticeable limp.

"Hop," he said, extending his hand. I noticed the last joint on his index finger was missing.

"Axe," I said. "I'm here to talk about a bear. Mr. Flark told me you used to be an animal trainer. I thought maybe you could help me."

"Sure. I'll try." He sat back down and pointed out a chair for me. Effie sat herself next to her husband on the couch.

"Maybe you know the bear I'm talking about. It's been troubling the Hatfield brothers."

"Sure, I've heard of that bear. It escaped from a circus?"

"That's the story we're telling the public. I can't say anything more. Do you suppose it's actually possible to train a bear to behave like an attack dog, or a bloodhound?"

"When I was training animals, I always said it depended on the beast. Some animals can be trained to do almost anything. And others, well, I think they just don't want to learn, don't want to cooperate. Bears are smart, and they've got a good sense of smell. I don't see why one couldn't be taught to seek out and kill someone. But, like I said, it depends on the beast."

"Did you ever train a bear?"

"Once. A spectacled bear. They call them that because they've got markings on their face that looks like they're wearing glasses. His name was

Ramsey, and he wasn't too cooperative. Kind of lazy. I could never get him to do much. We had a warthog, Calvin, who could do twice as many tricks as old Ramsey. Smart as a whip, and eager to learn. Wonder what ever happened to him?"

"Couldn't say. So, you think a bear might be trained to kill on command, so to speak. You've lived in this area a while?"

"Ten years."

I could hear kids yelling and laughing in another room.

"You've got kids?" I asked.

"Five," said Hop.

"If they're making too much noise I'll ask them to keep it down," said Effie.

"No, they're fine," I said. "Would either of you happen to know why anyone would want the Hatfield brothers dead?"

Neither of them spoke for a moment.

"They're tough customers," said Hop, finally. "I've had trouble with them myself. One of them shot a horse of ours. I think it was an accident, but they didn't want to replace the horse. I can't afford a lawyer. I figured I was just out of luck."

"You mean you weren't?"

"No. Cuthbert finally came through with the money. Paid me top dollar, too. Gave me more than I'd actually paid for the horse. But don't spread around what I just told you. I don't think Ambrose knows his brother paid me. That Ambrose is something. Hit me in the jaw, he did.

Knocked me down."

I looked at Hop. He was a little guy, with a very friendly face. Good old Ambrose.

"I'm glad things worked out for you," I said. "Can you think of anybody who might actually hate the Hatfields enough to murder them? I'm not asking you to rat on anybody, but I've got a job to do."

"You're not really looking for the bear, are you?" asked Effie. "You want to find the man who owns it."

"If it is a man. I know Ambrose and Cuthbert's ex-wives aren't any too fond of them."

"So what are you thinking?" asked Hop. "That one of those ladies hired me to train a killer bear for them?"

The guy was sharper than I thought.

"Not at all. Not at all. I don't think you have anything to do with that bear. I'm just consulting you as an expert in training wild animals."

"Not an expert. But compared to other folks around here? Sure, I'm the guy to suspect. But I'm telling you, the only animals I train now are horses."

I heard a dog bark in the kids' room. So that's where the dog was.

"I believe you," I said. "I'm just looking for information."

"I think you've pumped me dry," said Hop. He stood up. He still looked friendly, but I knew I'd worn out my welcome.

"I'm sorry to have taken up so much of your time. Thanks for the information. I can find my way out."

Effie escorted me anyway.

"Hop wouldn't have anything to do with a crazy plan like that," she told me.

"No one's accusing your husband of anything. Set your mind at rest."

I headed back to the Hatfield's. They'd be getting ready to turn in by the time I got there, and I had some questions. I wanted to talk to Cuthbert about his ex-wife.

In spite of having had a nap, I was pretty ready for bed myself. The big house was still lit up when I arrived. I parked the truck next to the Hatfield's Jimmy and went inside, filled a cup with coffee from the big speckled pot on the hearth, and strolled over to watch the brothers play checkers.

"Find anything out?" asked Ambrose.

"Not much. Mr. Carlson hasn't worked as an animal trainer for years. And that little mom and pop zoo he worked at didn't have anything much more exotic than dancing chickens. Still, it was worth a shot."

"Your leg work doesn't seem to add up to much," complained Ambrose.

"He's doing the best he can," said Cuthbert. "He knows what he's doing, I'm sure."

I appreciated his defense of me.

"Any more bear sightings?" I asked.

"No," said Cuthbert." We haven't been out

since dark. Ambrose is fixing to go out and look around."

"By himself?" I asked.

"That's how he wants it," said Cuthbert. "He thinks you and me make too much noise."

"I don't think that's a good idea," I told Ambrose.

"Your job isn't to look out for me. Your job is to get to the bottom of this bear mess. I'll have my rifle. I'll be fine."

"That's an awfully big bear," I said.

"Not as big as you probably think," said Ambrose. "You were scared, that's all. Cuthbert and me have shot bigger bears than old Reaper."

"That a fact?"

"Hell, I'll show you. Come see our little game room."

The "game" room was located just off of the living room. There was a second fireplace, cold, a table, and a couple of chairs. The walls were fairly covered with the heads of elk and deer, with huge racks. On the floor was a bearskin rug with the head still attached. I had to admit it looked gigantic.

"Cuthbert shot that fellow about four years ago. Took three bullets. It weighed out at close to five-hundred pounds. Biggest black bear we'd ever seen."

"Is it a cross-breed like the Reaper?"

"No. Just a very big black. Pretty old, I imagine. Look at its teeth. They're worn down some."

I went over and bent down to examine the dead beast's dental attributes. Those big teeth looked plenty sharp to me. Ambrose came over and patted the bear's head affectionately.

"This bruin almost took my brother," he said, then frowned. "Cuthbert, you've got to change that bandage of yours more often. You been bleeding in here." He pointed out a couple of reddish-brown spots on the pine-wood floor.

"What?" said Cuthbert, "I haven't been bleeding in here. Why would I even come into this room?"

"How do you explain these blood stains?"

Cuthbert went over and looked.

"Well, maybe I was in here. I don't remember. Leg's mostly healed now."

"What happened exactly?" I asked. "Reaper chased you up a tree and then climbed up after you?"

"That's right. I was by myself. Ambrose was off in town, checking on his sons. It was broad daylight. I had my rifle with me, though.

"Old Reaper came out of nowhere and charged me. I jumped into a tree and he climbed right up after me. He grabbed onto my leg and I got my rifle unslung. As soon as I got my gun in my hands, the Reaper dropped back down to the ground and took off. I got off a shot, but I missed."

"When I got back home," said Ambrose, "Cuthbert was on the living room floor, bleeding. I patched him up. I had to stitch him up some."

"You guys ever hear of a doctor?"

"Closest doctor is an hour's drive away. Folks up here learn how to patch up themselves."

"It shook me some," said Cuthbert. "I hate to admit it, but I was as shook as a baby rabbit. My hat fell off when I was up that tree. I went back later to find it, and damned if I could even find the tree I'd climbed! I looked around for half-an-hour and didn't even find my tracks. Or the bear's."

Ambrose laughed, a jarring sound.

"We can't all be brave, brother," he said. "Speaking of which, I guess it's time for me to go out hunting for the Reaper."

We went back into the living room. Ambrose pulled on his coat, grabbed up his thirty-ought-six, and left the cabin without so much as a good bye. Cuthbert stirred up the fire, poured himself a big whiskey, and settled into a chair.

"Sure you don't want any whiskey?" he asked. "Never been around a man who drinks so little."

"I'll stick to my coffee. Tell me about your ex-wife, Cuthbert."

"Melinda? What do you want to know about her for?"

"She's a suspect. So is your brother's ex-wife, Kelly."

"Shoot, those girls don't know how to train bears. I can see Kelly running over Ambrose with her car, or shooting him, but she couldn't train no bear."

"Someone could train it for her."

"Maybe. But she wouldn't bother. She's fixed OK. She don't have to see Ambrose much. Her kids are living with her, and she's got some money. She's satisfied."

"What about Melinda?"

"She don't hate me so much. It's not like with Ambrose and Kelly."

"What happened to your marriage? Why'd it go sour?"

"Lots of reasons, I reckon. I wouldn't say this if Ambrose was here — and don't you tell him — but he poisoned my marriage."

"Oh? How so?"

"Ambrose busted up with his wife first, then he moved in with me and Melinda and the boys. Hell, I don't know why he couldn't have found another place to stay. He could have moved up here, but he was still working then. We both were."

"You ever miss working? Ever get tired of just your brother for company? Checkers, squirrel stew, and whiskey — is that enough of a life for you?"

"I've got my boys. I see them when I can. And then we've got our hobby of stuffing birds. But, yeah, I sometimes miss working. Some of the boys I worked with weren't bad. I don't see any of them anymore."

"How did Ambrose poison your marriage?"

"He was always hanging around, scarcely left the house. He and Melinda didn't get along, and

Ambrose kept telling me I was henpecked. He said I needed to take the upper hand.

"I think he meant I should use my fists on my wife. I don't believe in that kind of thing. Dad did it to Mom, and Granddaddy did it to Granny, but I never thought it was the right thing to do. I never did hit Melinda, and I didn't take the strap to my boys the way Ambrose did with his sons.

"He just kept riding me about it. And then Melinda started nagging me about Ambrose living with us. She kept saying I should act like a man and throw him out, make him find someplace else to live. It got to where the three of us were arguing all the time. It was hard on Bret and Cory, my boys.

"Finally, it just looked like the best thing was for me to leave. And then Melinda said she wanted a divorce."

"Sounds like a mess."

"Sure enough."

7

Ambrose returned to the cabin after about half-an-hour. He hadn't seen the Reaper. He seemed disappointed.

"The sooner that bear's dead, the sooner things can get back to normal." He gave me a hard look. "You going to do something besides talk to folks?"

"I'm not going to kill that bear, if that's what you're talking about. I'll do my job the way I've always done it. I've had some success."

"I reckon you know what you're doing," said Cuthbert. "Boys, it's bedtime."

We said our goodnights and I headed over to the little cabin. I had Ben's six-shooter in my paw the whole way. The cabin was cold. It seemed almost colder than the outdoors. I piled the wood stove full of kindling and lit it with a kitchen match.

After a time, the place became a little less glacial. I crawled into bed, pulled the quilt and the army blankets over my head, and tried to go to sleep. I succeeded for the most part. But, once again, I woke up a couple of times thinking I'd heard chuffing sounds outside my windows and claws on the walls of the cabin. I hoped it was my over-active imagination.

Next morning's breakfast consisted of eggs, elk sausage, and more flapjacks. After we'd eaten, I told Ambrose and Cuthbert that I wanted to call Tracy.

"I hope I'm not overstepping my bounds as your humble guest, boys, but I wouldn't mind a little privacy when I make my phone call. I'm a newlywed, remember?"

They both snorted and laughed about that, but they put on their coats and went out to look for signs of the Reaper. They left me alone for half an hour. I gave Tracy a quick call to tell her I'd be coming to town, and would stop by to see her when I could. However, the real reason I wanted privacy was to call the Hatfield's sister, Bethany, and get the phone numbers for Kelly and Melinda. It was way too early for phone calls, but I hoped Bethany would be up. She wasn't. A very sleepy, though seductive, voice answered the phone.

"Hello? Is this an emergency?"

"No. This is Axe Hatchett. Listen, I hate to bother you this early in the morning, but this is the only chance I've had to call you."

"It's all right. I'm awake now. It's almost time for me to get up anyway. I've got to get the girls off to school. How can I help you?"

"I was wondering if you could give me the phone numbers for Kelly and Melinda."

Her laugh came through the phone like ambrosia poured over cracked ice. "Why do you want to talk to them? Are they suspects?"

"Everybody's a suspect in my line of business. I just want to talk to them, ask them a few questions."

"I'll give you Melinda's number, but she'll be at work most of the day. Kelly and I are having lunch today. We're friends. She probably wouldn't mind if you joined us, if you're interested."

"That'd be swell. I always like to look at people when I talk to them."

"We're meeting at the Gypsy Wagon at twelve. Do you know where it is?"

"I think so. Downtown. What kind of food do they serve?"

"They serve tea and little sandwiches and fancy desserts. Does that sound like your kind of place?"

"Can I get a greasy cheese burger there?"

She treated me to another laugh. "Maybe a very tiny cheeseburger, with a frou-frou toothpick stuck in it."

"That'll have to do, I guess. I'll see you at twelve."

I called Melinda next. She answered on the first ring.

"Yes?"

"Is this Melinda Hatfield?"

"I don't go by that name anymore."

"My name's Axe Hatchett. I'm a private investigator working for the Hatfield brothers."

"Lucky you."

"I'd like to talk to you, if I may, about your ex-husband and your former brother-in-law."

"Why?"

"Just part of my investigation. There's a bear trying to kill them."

"I hope it eats both of them. Cuthbert told me something about that bear when he talked to me on the phone the other day. What do I have to do with it?"

"I'm sure you have nothing to do with it. I'd just like to chat with you, that's all."

"I'm almost out the door. I've got to go to work."

"Where are the kids?"

"At Grandma's. Is that any of your business?"

"Is there a number where I can reach you later?"

"I can't take calls at work. I'm a factory girl. Call me at home this evening, if you must."

She hung up. So much for Melinda. Ambrose and Cuthbert returned in a little bit. They'd found bear tracks, but hadn't seen the bear.

"Who are the Carlson's closest neighbors?" I asked the brothers.

"That'd be the Stewarts and old man Grimpen," said Cuthbert.

"Their numbers are likely in the phone book," said Ambrose.

"That's OK. I like taking people by surprise. Can you tell me how to get to their places?"

"I can draw you a map," said Ambrose.

More damned maps.

I headed out to the truck, armed with a map drawn on the back of a phone bill envelope. I hadn't scraped the crabgrass off of my face, but I figured it made me look like one of the locals.

The Studebaker was slow to start. It was a damned cold morning and it felt like snow was coming. I needed to get my detective chores done before a storm closed the road.

I drove to the Stewart's home first. They lived in a fairly new log house with two junked trucks in the front yard. The door was answered by a pretty, pregnant woman who told me her husband wasn't home.

"That's all right. I can talk to you. My name's Axe Hatchett. I'm doing a little investigating for the Hatfield brothers. I'm looking for a bear."

She almost slammed the door in my face.

"Listen, Mrs. Stewart, this bear is dangerous."

"So are the Hatfield brothers, especially that Ambrose."

"I won't disagree with you, but I'm here to talk about the bear."

"I don't know anything about any bear. Is it a pet of theirs'?"

"Quite the contrary. It's trying to kill them."

She made a disgusted noise and rolled her lovely eyes. "I wish it all the luck in the world."

"Can I come in? You're letting a lot of heat out your front door."

"OK. Come on in."

I entered a neat little living room. There were some children's toys on the floor but no kids in sight. Maybe they were at school already. Mrs. Stewart showed me to a chair but didn't offer me coffee. She took a seat herself.

"Hank hates Ambrose," Mrs. Stewart started off. She frowned and chewed on a fingernail.

I decided that maybe I wasn't here to talk about a bear after all.

"Why is that?" I said.

"Ambrose can't leave a married woman alone. I kept running into him in town, in the grocery store mostly. He's a masher. He wouldn't stop pestering me. I told Hank, and he went right over to the Hatfield place and picked a fight. Hank's pretty good sized — he played football in high school — but Ambrose mopped up the floor with him.

"Hank hates him like the devil. Worst of all, Hank thinks maybe I took a shine to Ambrose. There's nothing in that. I can't stand the man. But, Hank, he's not always good with his head. He thinks maybe I was stepping out on him. He thinks maybe this baby ain't his."

"I'm sorry. That must be terrible for you."

"I'll say. And it's that damned Ambrose's fault. I think he maybe said something about me to Hank. Like he was sleeping with me or something.

Why would you want to work for folks like that?"

"A man's got to do something for a living. I'm sorry you hate the Hatfields, but I can see why. Now, about this bear. It wanders around. Have you seen a big bear in your neighborhood lately? He's a kind of a brownish-gold. And he's got a hump on his back like a grizzly, but he's likely not one. Just a big black bear."

"We haven't seen any bears around here. A month or two ago, maybe, I saw a little black bear, not even full grown. Couldn't have weighed more than a hundred pounds. And it was black."

"All right. Let me ask you something else. You live just up the road from the Carlson's. Mr. Carlson has a horse trailer. Have you seen his truck pulling that trailer a lot lately?"

She shook her head impatiently.

"What do horses have to do with a bear? I don't spend much time looking out the window. And I can't even see the road from our house."

"OK. Thanks." I stood up. "I think your husband is a fool to doubt your fidelity. And I hope when the baby's born it looks just like him."

"You and me both."

I went out to my truck and drove down the lousy dirt road some more. Old man Grimpen's place was about a mile past the Carlson homestead. It was a neat little frame house that was painted white with green trim. An old but clean pickup truck was parked in a car port. There were flower boxes, sans flowers, under the windows, and a swing on the porch. I exited my vehicle, stepped onto the porch, and rattled the shiny brass knocker. In a minute, the door opened.

"Yes? Can I help you? Have you lost your way, young fellow?"

In spite of the "young fellow," and the moniker "Old Man Grimpen," the man who opened the door couldn't have been more than forty. He was a dapper little fellow, dressed in new jeans with creases in them, a collared shirt, and a fancy sweater.

"Mr. Grimpen?"

"That's me. I guess you aren't lost after all. Come in. Coffee?"

There was a polite little terrier sitting on the living room carpet. A cheery fire burned in the stone fireplace. The room was neat and spotless. It only needed doilies to make it look like Grandma's place. I sat down in a flower-printed chair that was offered.

"My name's Axe Hatchett. I'm a private investigator. I'm doing a little work for the Hatfield brothers. Do you know them?"

"By reputation. And not a very good reputation."

"They're having some trouble right now with a marauding bear. It's already tried to kill one of the brothers, and it wanders around a lot. Have you by any chance seen it in your neighborhood?" I described the Reaper.

"Why, no, I haven't seen such a bear. I'm sure

I'd remember it. I've seen raccoons, and a fox or two, and squirrels, and skunks. Birds of all sorts, of course."

"Let me ask you something else. You live down the road from the Carlson's. Have you seen Mr. Carlson's horse trailer a whole lot of times in the last two or three months?"

"What an unusual question. Do you think he's hauling bears in it? I do see the Carlson's horse trailer quite often. Mr. Carlson does a little repair and carpentry work in his spare time. He uses the horse trailer as a sort of utility vehicle sometimes. You know, to haul lumber, shingles, and such. But I've never seen bears in his trailer."

"Just asking. Do you have any particular beef with the Hatfields?"

"Me? No. I stay out of their way. It seems a wise practice. I've heard stories, many of them. But, no, I have no beef with them."

"Tell me some of those stories."

"I'd just be passing on gossip and I don't want to do that."

I stood up.

"Thank you for your time, and for the coffee, Mr. Grimpen. Say, what do you do for a living?"

"I'm a retired bookkeeper."

"You're pretty young to be retired."

"I started working at a very early age. And I've made some fairly prudent investments."

"Well, thanks again."

I patted the dog on the head as Grimpen led me

to the door. While I'd been inside, toasting my toes and sipping good coffee, it had started to snow outside. The flakes were pretty big and coming down hard. I decided I better hurry up and get to town if I was going to have any chance of returning to the Hatfields that day.

I have to admit, I was as happy as a spring worm when I turned the corner and saw the white-brick building that housed my office, the sandwich shop, and the apartment Tracy and I share. It was great to be back home. I parked the truck at the curb and went into the sandwich shop. Tracy was standing behind the counter. It was too late for breakfast and too early for lunch, so the place wasn't crowded.

Tracy squealed like a kid. She ran over, threw her arms around me, and gave me a sloppy kiss.

"The prodigal son has returned," she said.

"Where's my fatted calf?"

"In your arms. Or we've got sandwiches, if you'd rather."

"I had a big breakfast, and I'm meeting some folks for lunch."

She narrowed her eyes.

"Dames?"

"Just doing my job, Tracy."

"Are these floozies good looking?"

"I've only met one of them. She's not bad, if you like Ava Gardner types."

"And of course you don't."

"I like your type. In fact, I love you."

"You know, sometimes I miss the way you used to insult me. Do you ever miss my not insulting you? I never meant anything by it."

"We'll get back to trading insults. But it will take time."

Ben and Allie came out from behind the counter to greet me.

"So, the truck — it runs fine?" asked Ben.

"Yes. Like a top. Thanks again for the loan. Tracy's Chevy wouldn't have a chance on those roads."

"It's our Chevy now," Tracy said. "Since we don't have the Ruby Roadrunner anymore."

"I'm sorry we had to sell the Nash, sweet meat, but we needed the cash."

"I know, and it's OK. We don't need two cars. How's the case going?"

I told her and Ben and Allie what was going on with the bear investigation.

"You think that Hop Carlson guy trained the bear and sicced it on the Hatfields?" Tracy asked.

"He's got to be involved in it somehow, I know that. And I can't believe that anyone who isn't really close to the Hatfield brothers would come up with such an unusual way to kill them. It sounds like a family matter to me. That's why I'm having lunch with the Hatfields' sister and Ambrose's ex-wife. I hope to talk to Cuthbert's ex-wife as well."

"You know, Axe," said Ben, "if you're going back to the mountains today, and it is snowing, I can help you to make the truck drive better."

"How's that?"

"Sand bags. We keep a couple of bags of the sand in our garage. When it is snowy, or icy, I put the sand bags in the truck bed."

"Good idea."

"If you would like, I give you the key to our garage and you can go get the bags of the sand." The rotund Ben fished keys out of his pocket and dropped them into my palm.

"That'd be swell."

"Make sure you come back before you go to lunch," said Tracy.

"I will. I've got plenty of time."

"Be careful when you're driving in the mountains with snow," Allie said. "You must take care of yourself. Think of your Tracy."

"I'm always thinking of her."

Ben gave me directions to the Ozhammer house, and he didn't need to draw a damned map. I drove over and fetched the sand bags and wrestled them into the bed of the Studebaker. I went back to the sandwich shop, spent a little more time with Tracy, then headed off for my lunch at the Gypsy Wagon.

8

The restaurant was housed in an unspeakably cute little Victorian house near the main downtown area. Both Bethany and Kelly were waiting for me. They were sitting at a little glass-topped table somewhat bigger than a hubcap when I joined them.

Bethany was dressed up today in a print dress that no-doubt enjoyed molding itself to her graceful curves. Her hair was down and nicely framed her beautiful face.

Kelly wasn't bad either. She was a frosty-eyed blonde with long limbs and a come-hither glare.

"We've already ordered," said Bethany, gesturing at my menu. "Kelly, this is Mr. Hatchett, the detective who's tracking down my brothers' bothersome bear."

"It can't be bothersome enough, Mr. Hatchett," said Kelly, in a throaty voice with plenty of ice in it. "Bethany tells me you want to talk to me about Ambrose. What do you want to know about the worthless s.o.b.?"

"Oh, this and that. Why you married him, why you divorced him, why you might want to kill him."

She laughed, which was an invitation to cringe.

"You're not a cop. Do you mean to tell me you think I've hired a bear to kill my husband? If I was a bear, I'd find something more appetizing to chew on than dear unwashed Ambrose."

"I don't figure anybody hired the bear He'd probably work for treats. Seriously, if this bear business gets any worse, every one of your husband's enemies — and I hear there are legions — will be on the suspect list."

"How dramatic," said Kelly. "I've got nothing to worry about. I have the perfect alibi. I ignore Ambrose like he doesn't even exist. He doesn't cross my mind. No one who knows me would believe I was trying to kill him. Certainly not with a trick bear."

"You must see him some of the time. You share sons."

"When I see him, I treat him like a meter reader or the paper boy. I pay as little attention to him as possible."

"But it wasn't always that way. You shared years with him as his wife. Is it true he beat you?"

Kelly looked shocked, angry. That's what I was hoping for.

"Hey, no rough stuff," warned Bethany. "No tough-guy detective tricks. Understand? Kelly's had all the rough behavior she can take."

"Sorry. I like to get right to the point."

"Yes," said Kelly, "he beat me. And I let him, for a while. Then I divorced him, and I've got big fat alimony and child support checks to show just what I did to him in court."

"I heard he fought you pretty hard with a big fat lawyer."

"Sure, but it didn't work out like he was hoping. The judge took my side. Why wouldn't he? Ambrose wasn't even working by the time we went to court. He admitted having beat me and the kids, though he didn't put it that way. He said it'd been necessary to discipline us, which is what any good husband and father would do.

"Then there were the affairs. I hired a guy like you, only even sleazier. He collected plenty of evidence of my husband's affairs. I came out fine, money-wise. I got the kids. I got my pound of flesh. I'm through with Ambrose. When the kids are grown, I'll never see the guy again."

"That's really how it is," said Bethany. "Kelly hardly ever mentions Ambrose to me, unless I mention him first. I'm surprised she even has anything to do with me."

"Come on, Bethany, you aren't your brother. You're the good Hatfield. The smart Hatfield."

"I'm still my brothers' kid sister. That won't change."

"Just don't bring them around me. OK?" said Kelly.

"What about me, Mr. Hatchett?" Bethany said. "Am I a suspect? I did kill my husband. And I grew up with Ambrose and Cuthbert, who were never exactly saints. Maybe I want to be rid of them."

"You wouldn't benefit much from their deaths, as I understand it. They're leaving all their money and property to your nephews."

"Good for them. I'm glad," said Bethany.

"But it doesn't leave you much of a motive as a murder suspect."

"I'm broken-hearted."

I looked at my menu. Some of it was in phony French. I looked around the restaurant to see what other people were eating. Tiny quartered slices of bread, with the crusts removed, made into sandwiches with fillings as thin as a mugged man's wallet. I figured I'd have to order twelve of everything just to end up with a decent belly's worth of food.

The waitress arrived, wearing a frilly apron the size of a two-cent stamp, and a hat to match, and took my order. Black coffee, two Monte Christos, and a cheese plate.

"Do you serve fries?" I asked.

The frail waif gave me a look that let me know the Gypsy Wagon would serve fries over her dead body. I shrugged.

"But tell me, Mr. Hatchett," said Bethany, "what have you learned so far about the bear that's trying to eat my dear brothers?"

"I've seen him. He's big, fast, and he doesn't appear to be entirely tame. He chased me and your brothers up some trees the other night. The Reaper's not a normal bear, I'll tell you that."

"The Reaper?" asked Kelly, biting into a sandwich with some kind of pink filling.

"That's what Ambrose and Cuthbert call him," I said. "Like the Grim Reaper, only fuzzy. They're scared of him, and for good reason. Cuthbert's already been mauled by the thing, though Ambrose played doctor and patched him up," I said.

"Dear kindly Ambrose," said Kelly, acid dripping from her dewy pink lips.

"I still don't know why the Forest Service hasn't been able to do anything about the situation," said Bethany. "Isn't animal control part of their job?"

"They tried, but the bear disappeared on them. Same thing happened with a professional hunting guide they hired. This is a smart bear. That's why I believe he had to be trained. I've even met someone who could have trained him. Either he's working on his own hook, or somebody's hired him to provide a very scary murder weapon."

"Somebody like me?" asked Kelly.

"Somebody who not only doesn't like your ex-husband and his brother, but also wants to play with them. Who knows where this bear comes from? He might have cost money. It would cost money to pay the trainer. Someone's going to a lot of trouble and expense, and they're having fun while they're doing it. Who could it be?"

"The whole business is crazy," said Bethany.

"Can either of you think of anyone you know, or the Hatfield brothers know, who would want to play a game like this?"

"No," said Kelly.

"Me neither," said Bethany.

"Listen, ladies, lunch is on me."

"I can't let you do that, Mr. Hatchett," said Bethany.

"I pay for my own lunches," said Kelly.

"It's like this," I said. "The price of this lunch gets added to the expenses for my investigation. I'll be handing the bill to Ambrose."

"Deal," said Kelly. "Let me order dessert, and something to go."

I hadn't learned much from the ladies. I hoped I'd have better luck with Melinda. It was way too early to call her again, so I headed home. The snow was getting thicker. If it was snowing this hard in town, then it was no doubt snowing harder in the mountains. I stuck my ugly face into Ben And Allie's Sandwich Shop and the counter girl kissed it.

"You're back," said Tracy. "Were those dames good to you?"

"Why wouldn't they be?"

"I was hoping they'd throw you out on your ear."

"They did, but I've still got one good ear left, and it's for you."

Ben came over. "The Studebaker, do the sand

bags help it to drive?"

"Didn't slide around a bit. But this snow's getting bad. I might have to stay home tonight."

"That would be so awful," said Tracy, smiling. "Right in the middle of a case, too."

"I can live with it," I said, "if you can."

The shop wouldn't close until six, so Tracy had a few more hours to work. There were still a few customers coming in for late lunches, and the place was busy enough that I was just in the way. I told Tracy I'd be upstairs in our apartment if she wanted me. I needed a nap.

"I'm sure it's hard sleeping with bears around," she said. "Have a good nap. Wish I could join you."

I went upstairs and tried to sleep, but it was no good. The kittens climbed all over me and mewed, then got bored with their dad and climbed onto the dresser to knock stuff onto the floor. I began wondering what kind of delinquents they were growing up to be. Mayhew, the mean orange one, seemed to egg on Eben, the uglier cream one, who's a gentler soul by nature. Kids, what are you going to do with them?

Thoughts kept festering in my head. One of them was pretty crazy. but sometimes those are the good ones. I got up, grabbed the phone, and called the Hatfield number. Cuthbert answered.

"Hello! Hatfields'!"

"Cuthbert? This is Axe. How's the summer weather up there?"

"Well, it's stopped snowing. I don't know what the roads are like. They won't plow until morning at the earliest. Our county's not the richest, and the plowing doesn't always get done that quick."

"But I could make it up there early in the morning?"

"Don't see why not. You'll not be here for supper then? We're having porcupine."

"I'm tempted to come up tonight, just for the food, but I think it will have to wait. I'll likely see you both in the morning."

"Fine. How's the case going?"

"Oh, I have an idea or two. Nothing definite."

"Well, keep working on it. See you in the morning. You'll be here for breakfast?"

"Not that early. Save some of that porcupine for me, and a quill to pick my teeth with. Good bye."

It was still too early to call Melinda. If the idea I was ruminating on was correct, then calling her wasn't that important. I thought about how much Cuthbert might hate Ambrose. He blamed his brother for his failed marriage. And he was obviously going around trying to undo some of Ambrose's rotten behavior. Then there was the little matter of Ambrose treating his brother badly at times. But did Cuthbert have enough hate in him to actually try to kill Ambrose? And to use a trick bear to do it? I hoped I'd be finding out pretty soon.

I went downstairs and into the sandwich shop. Business was booming, but the four of us handled it easily. Around five, things started slowing down. The early supper crowd was breaking up, and the place closed at six.

At the end of the day, there were always sandwiches that had been made up earlier. Ben and Allie took some of these home for their own family, but they were kind enough to give me and Tracy a few. We never knew what we would get. This evening it was ham and cheese, roast beef and Swiss, and corn beef and onion. Tracy and I took our food upstairs and ate it at our own little dining table.

"I keep thinking of that bear," said Tracy, around a mouthful of sandwich. She'd taken her funny cap off, and her hair was sticking up. I rumpled it some more for her.

"That bear's not going to get me, if that's what you're thinking," I said, dunking some bread and corned beef into my coffee. "I'm a tough guy, remember?"

"You're not tougher than a bear. If it chews your legs off, don't come running to me. Sometimes I wish you had a safer job."

"Like a zoo keeper?"

"No. Maybe you could get work as a mail sorter or something."

"Then I'd die of boredom. Might as well get shot, or mauled by a bear."

"Don't make jokes, you big sap. I worry about you. I paid good money for your wedding ring."

"I'll be very, very, careful. I promise. I'll let the

Hatfields handle the Reaper. They've got rifles and they know how to shoot."

We finished our meal and I called Melinda.

"Hello?"

"Axe Hatchett again."

"Oh, you. I'm trying to get dinner on the table for my kids."

"Let me ask you one question. How much does Cuthbert hate Ambrose?"

"What? They're brothers. Cuthbert doesn't hate him. Though he ought to. Ambrose runs rough-shod over him, but Cuthy just takes it. He doesn't have a lot of spine."

"What about you? Do you have hostile feelings for either brother?"

"I'm over all that. I don't have time. I made a mistake, and then I unmade it. Simple as that. Why are you asking?"

"I'm just a curious guy. Thanks for talking to me."

"That's it?"

"That's it. I hope you aren't disappointed."

I hung up.

"Who was that?" Tracy asked. "Another doll?"

"Never set eyes on the woman."

"You're acting funny, like when you have an idea. Spill."

"I'm thinking one of the brothers might want to kill the other."

"That sounds crazy."

"It's a crazy world. You want to split that last

sandwich?"

We spent a quiet evening together and a very pleasant night. I was up way early the next morning. Tracy and I had a quick breakfast, and I headed for the Studebaker.

"Why you rushing off?" asked Tracy. "Don't you like your new wife anymore?"

"More than ever. But I've got work to do."

I kissed her good bye, promised to call, and headed for the high lonesome.

9

The roads were pretty bad. In spite of the sand bags in the back of the truck, I had a hard time getting traction at times. But I made it. I arrived at the big house well after breakfast time. The brothers were having more coffee and were indulging in an early game of checkers. Spotty and Doc were stretched out under the table. They didn't even get up to look me over.

"Any sign of the Reaper?" I asked.

Cuthbert had saved me a little of the porcupine stew. It had peas and carrots in it, and some unnamable herbs. I shoveled it in on top of my breakfast, and damned if it wasn't pretty tasty.

"We're going out to look for tracks," Ambrose told me. "Want to come with us?"

"I just got in out of the cold. I'll stay here and make a couple of phone calls, if you don't mind."

"You just came from your sweetie," he said. "You're not lonely already, are you?"

"I've got other folks to call. I'm working."

"We didn't hear nothing from the Reaper last night," Cuthbert said. "Maybe he's gone."

"We couldn't be that lucky," said Ambrose. "He'll hang around until we're both in his belly. But not if I get another shot at him."

"Good luck." I said.

The brothers put on their coats, Ambrose grabbed up his rifle, and the two headed out the door with the dogs. Alone at last. I called Bethany. She answered the phone with her usual throaty purr.

"This is Axe," I told her. "I've got a screwy question for you, and don't bite my head off if you don't like it."

"OK. You've warned me. What's the question, Mr. Detective?"

"Any chance one of your brothers hates the other one enough to want him dead?"

"Interesting question. They're both hot-tempered, and living together like they do, I'd say they have more than their share of fights. Ambrose tends to pick on Cuthbert. And I know Ambrose thinks Cuthbert tries to run Ambrose's life in his own quiet way. Are you asking me if there's enough bad blood between them that one of them would hire a trained bear to kill the other?"

"It's just a goofy idea I had. Since Cuthbert's already been attacked by the Reaper, I figure Ambrose might be the one who hired the trained bear. Your older brother is a pretty hard guy to get along with."

"He is, but he doesn't murder people, as far as I know. I think you're on the wrong trail. Somebody other than one of my brothers is behind this bear nightmare."

"So, you don't like my idea?"

"I'm sure you can come up with better ones."

"I'll try. I'm thinking of calling up Harvey Rundell and picking his brain a bit. He's still a pretty good suspect."

"I'd put my money on him any day."

"OK. Well, thanks for the chat."

I hung up and started looking around for a phone book so I could call Rundell, but I was interrupted by some shouting outside. Was I too late? Had Cuthbert already sicced the bear on his brother?

The front door burst open. It was Ambrose, looking crazy. There were flecks of fresh blood on the front of his coat.

"It's Cuthbert!" he shouted, standing in the open door. "He's been killed! The Reaper got him."

I was properly stunned. I stood up and grabbed Ambrose's arm. He dropped his rifle and it clattered to the floor.

"Are you sure he's dead?" I asked. "Let's go look."

"Dead? His throat's torn out!"

"Let's go look,"

I pulled on my coat and we both went out the door. I grabbed Ben's thumb-buster from my pocket. The big man led me on a run out into the woods. We came to a spot where the snow was all tracked up. Cuthbert lay on his back, most of his throat and neck gone. Part of his face was gone, too. The fresh snow was stained with dark blood everywhere.

Doc sat off to the side, whining, and Spotty came slinking out of the trees. They looked as depressed as two dogs can.

"Call the hospital and the cops," I commanded.

"Too late."

"It's not too late to call the cops."

He thought about it. "I'm going after that bear," he said, and he actually turned and started off on the bear's trail without his rifle. The guy was shook up.

"Wait!" I shouted. "We can't leave your brother's body out here. Help me carry him to the house."

He hesitated, then came back. He stooped to lift his brother's body by the armpits. I took the feet. Dead men weigh a ton. They seem to gain weight as soon as the life oozes out of them. It took us forever to get Cuthbert back to the cabin. We laid him down on the living room floor and Ambrose covered him with an army blanket.

"I'm going out to get that bear," Ambrose told me. "Call the cops if you want, and wait here."

He grabbed up his rifle from the floor and went back out into the cold.

I called the cops and told them what was going

on. I warned them about the roads, and promised to stay right where I was. Cuthbert and I kept each other company for close to an hour. I had some coffee and lit a cigar.

Sometimes I'm an idiot. I should have reported Hop as soon as I suspected him of training the Reaper. I wondered, idly, what the bear's real name was. I called Tracy.

"I've got bad news," I told her. "Cuthbert Hatfield is dead, killed by the Reaper. Your new husband has failed again."

"Don't say that. You can't always keep murders from happening. Are you all right?"

"Sure. I'm just waiting for the cops to show up. I asked them to send some homicide guys. I hope they listen to me. This isn't just some unfortunate backwoods accident. It's murder all right."

"Is Ambrose the killer? Maybe he owns the trained bear."

"That's what I was thinking. He could kill his pet bruin and there would never be a case against him. Maybe you can help me solve this case, doll."

"I'm supposed to be your helpmate, in sickness and in health."

"Yeah, well, right now I'm feeling pretty sick. I don't like folks getting killed on my watch."

"You couldn't help it, molasses chew, but you can still track down the killer, whether it's Ambrose, or somebody else."

"I hope so."

I talked to her for a while longer, and then the

cops showed up. They arrived in a black Paddy wagon, which confused me. Then I realized that it might be the only vehicle they owned that could navigate these roads, especially through the snow. There were two uniformed officers, beefy guys, and the coroner. He looked as rumpled as always, and he had his constant companion, his pipe, clamped in his teeth. There was no homicide dick, and that annoyed me. The coroner lifted Cuthbert's blanket and said, "Died of a sore throat. Hope my kids don't get it."

He's a real cut-up, that coroner.

"How's come you didn't bring the homicide boys?" I asked.

"Cause it ain't a homicide," said one of the uniformed cops. The guy had a beer gut and his badge was pinned on crooked.

"It wasn't a wild bear. It was trained. Same as if somebody had trained a dog to kill someone."

"Maybe that's so, but it sounds screwy," said the other cop. "It ain't up to us, mister. We do what we're told." He turned to the coroner. "Doc, can we haul the stiff out to the truck now?"

"Wait a moment. Maybe he'll come around." He laughed sourly. "Sure, take him out to the wagon. He's not going to get any deader."

"You guys are at least going to talk to the dead man's brother, aren't you?" I asked.

"Where's his brother?" the first cop asked.

"Out in the woods trying to track down that bear."

"If he comes back soon, I'll talk to him, but it's beginning to snow again. I don't want to get stuck out here babysittin' a corpse. I'll take a statement from you, though. Wait until we're through loading the meat into the caboose, OK?"

"Whatever you say, officer."

I watched them carry Cuthbert out to the Paddy wagon. In fact, I followed them out the door. Something fell out of Cuthbert's coat pocket and the gendarmes didn't notice. I went over and picked it up. It was a dog whistle. What the hell? I stuck it in my pocket. I wasn't much in the mood for cooperating with the police.

Ambrose had apparently taken Spotty and Doc with him to track the bear. I wondered if he ever used a dog whistle on the mutts. Either that, or I hadn't been entirely wrong about Cuthbert. Surely, a dog whistle, or a bear whistle, could have been used with the Reaper. Hop would know. But if Cuthbert was the man who'd hired the trained bear, then it didn't make sense that the Reaper had attacked him.

Before Ambrose got back, the two cops grilled me, wrote down a bunch of unimportant stuff, and bade me a fond farewell. As they were leaving, I told them about Hop Carlson and his background. They said they'd look into it. Sure.

I was breathing fire over the absence of the homicide dicks. The guy with the crooked badge and the other one, a long drink of stale water with a bad attitude, didn't care. And the coroner was only interested in his pipe. The trio decided they couldn't wait to talk to Ambrose. They asked if I'd have him phone them. I said sure, why not?

"You boys have a nice ride down," I said.

I watched them lurch away into the thickening snowfall.

Left alone, I noticed some of Cuthbert's gore on the pine floor. I couldn't stand looking at it. I went into the kitchen and pumped some water into a bucket I found and played washerwoman. Ambrose still hadn't returned. I was getting antsy. There was nothing for me to do but sit around talking to myself. I decided to call Bethany.

"Hello?"

What a voice. It gave me a little spinal thrill. Then I remembered what I had to say to her.

"It's Axe Hatchett again. I've got some bad news for you."

"That's not good. Has something happened to Ambrose or Cuthbert?"

"Cuthbert." I couldn't make myself go on.

"What? Is it the bear? Tell me!"

"Cuthbert's dead. The bear got him. I don't think he could have suffered much."

"That damned Ambrose! He should have watched out for him."

I hadn't expected that.

"I'm sure Ambrose tried to protect his brother. He had his rifle with him. I don't have the whole story yet. I'll have to wait until he gets back. He's out hunting the bear."

"You've called the police? Where is Cuthbert? Where's his — body?"

"The police took it away. To the morgue, I imagine. Listen, I'm awfully sorry."

"Cuthbert was the good brother, if there was any decency left in either one of them. Find out what happened. You have to. Do you really believe the bear is trained?"

"I absolutely believe that. We're dealing with a murderer here. I'll do everything I can to find out who it is."

"Thank you," There were a lot of tears in her voice.

Ambrose picked that moment to come home. He walked into the front door with his shoulders slumped. When he saw me on the phone, he got red in the face.

"I'm talking to your sister," I said.

"Give me the phone."

Ambrose talked long and loud to his sister. To my surprise, his angry words were accompanied by an outpouring of tears. He practically blubbered. I stepped into the game room to give him some privacy, but I heard my name mentioned more than once, along with the endearing words: "damned worthless detective." He ended the phone call and came roaring through the house looking for me.

"You're fired!" he yelled when he found me amidst his hunting trophies. "Get your stuff packed up and clear out. My brother's dead because of you. And where is he? Where's Cuthbert's body?"

"The cops were here, along with the coroner. They took your brother to the morgue."

"Without my permission."

"They didn't need your permission. Listen, I'm sorry about your brother. It was a terrible way to die. I'll leave. Just let me get my things."

I tried to pass him in the doorway. He wouldn't let me. He grabbed a generous handful of my shirt collar and shook me. Then he pushed me away from him and aimed a roundhouse punch at my face with his right fist.

I dodged it, stepped forward, kicked his legs out from under him, and hurried into the living room. I grabbed up the rifle he'd left by the door, jacked all the shells out of it, and stuck it in a corner.

Ambrose lunged to his feet and came after me. I grabbed my overcoat and pulled Ben's revolver from it.

"Easy, big fellow," I warned. "There's already been one killing today. There's not going to be another. Calm down and I'll clear out. I'll send you a bill."

I was mad, though I shouldn't have been. The poor guy had just lost his brother.

"You won't get a cent out of me," he said. He'd stopped in the middle of the room. It looked like he wasn't going to bring the fight to me after all. "Hire any damned lawyer you want. I'm not paying you a dime."

I didn't bother to answer him. I left the big house and returned to the little cabin to fetch my suitcase and shotgun. Two minutes later, I was in the truck. It took a couple of minutes to get it started. Ambrose watched me from the open door of his house. I was glad to get away.

The drive back home took forever. Even with the windshield wipers going full tilt, the swirling snow made visibility almost impossible. The roads were slippery and I had to drive slowly.

My only thought was to get back to Tracy, have a cup of coffee, and find something to think about besides the Hatfield case. Of course, there was no case now. My services were no longer required. I was an out-of-work gumshoe again.

Some days are like that.

10

For the next couple of days I did nothing much. I played with Eben and Mayhew. They'd grown a lot since I'd given them to Tracy for Christmas. I then sat in my empty office and hoped for the phone to ring. When I got tired of that, I helped out in the sandwich shop when they wanted me. Tracy was awfully nice about it.

"You'll get more work," she assured me. "And you'll get your money form that Hatfield jerk. We'll hire a great big lawyer, bigger than anybody he can get."

"How are we going to pay for it?"

"It'll all work out. Quit worrying."

But I didn't. I kept worrying, and thinking. Cuthbert Hatfield had been murdered by a trained bear. I didn't have any doubts about that. The bear's behavior wasn't normal. The way it had eluded the forest service guys, and the professional hunter, didn't make sense, especially if the animal was wild and didn't have help.

The way it stalked the Hatfields, and no one else, wasn't normal either. I'd seen the animal myself, been chased up a tree by it, and there was something screwy about the way the beast had behaved.

Hop Carlson had to be behind its training. It would be too much of a coincidence to have more than one former wild animal trainer in the same part of the mountains. But was he working alone? I couldn't help myself. Paycheck or no paycheck, I had to try to solve Cuthbert's murder. On the evening of my second day home, I told Tracy my plan.

"I can't keep thinking about it," I told her. "Listen, I'm not working on anything else right now, so I might as well keep snooping around."

"Why don't you let the cops handle it?"

"Because they won't do a damned thing. They don't even think it was a homicide."

"They might have changed their minds. Why don't you find out?"

"The cops won't talk to me."

"Call your old neighbor. What's her name? Blythe Bliss."

That was a swell idea, and I should have thought of it myself. Officer Bliss, of the Quartz Quarry Police Department, had lived next door to me before Tracy and I had found our new apartment. I'd done her a favor or two, and she sometimes gave me a bit of police news that wasn't for public consumption. I gave her a call.

"Howdy," she answered. She's from west Texas.

"This is Axe. How's my former neighbor?"

"Lonely. I miss you watching me drink beer in the evenings. How's the kittens?"

Blythe's ugly tabby had given birth to our two ornery boys.

"They're doing great, getting into everything."

"How's married life?"

"Swell. You should try it."

"Not this girl. Did you just call up to chat, or are you fishing for police gossip?"

"Well, as a matter of fact — "

"I thought so. What do you want to know?"

"I just spent a couple of days up in the mountains, near Flinders Cone. A man was killed up there, attacked by a bear. I think it was murder."

"You're always thinking that. Bears can't be murderers — they can only be killers. You've got to be a person to be a murderer. That's how it works."

"Sure, but I think this bear was used as a murder weapon."

"Listen, I know the accident you're talking about. Seems like the dead man's brother thought the bear had been trained, like a fighting dog, to kill. Thought whoever owned the bear was targeting him and his brother. The police have looked into it at little, but there's no evidence that it's anything but a silly story. Besides, I think the Forest Service folks should be working on this."

"They are. At least, they were. But they don't have a homicide division, do they? I'm pretty certain this bear is somebody's pet. Not a very nice pet, but one that's been trained. I even gave the police the name of a guy up near the Hatfields — those are the guys who hired me — who used to train exotic animals for some mom and pop zoo in the south. His name's Hop Carlson. I think the cops should be talking to him."

"Honey, we've already talked to him. We searched his place, looking for any signs that he had a bear on his premises. We looked in his barn, his storage shed, his root cellar, and his horse trailer. We looked all around his property. There was no sign of a bear, not so much as a tuft of fur. He was pretty sore at us, and says he don't know a thing about that critter that killed Hatfield."

"That can't be true. I'm telling you. Are the cops going to keep looking into the matter?"

"I don't think so. We got two-legged murderers to worry about. Just put it out of your mind. Get some sleep. Play with the kittens."

"I've done all that. I'm telling you, Blythe, you're letting somebody get away with murder."

"Maybe so, but we can't go wasting time on every crack-pot tip we get from somebody like you."

"Oh, so I'm a crack-pot, am I?"

"A lovable one. Some of the time. If you want to prove that Hatfield fellow was a murder victim, you're going to have to supply the evidence yourself. You still on the case?"

"No. The remaining brother fired me."

"I'm sorry. You need to find another case to work on. Get your mind off or this bear malarkey."

"I'd be happy to get more work, but nobody's knocking down my office door to hire me."

"Things will pick up. Don't worry your pretty little head."

"It's not so pretty. Listen, it's been nice talking to you."

"It's good to hear your voice. Tell those kittens I said howdy. And that new wife of yours, too."

"I will. Good bye."

I got off the phone and looked at Tracy.

"No luck with the cops. They're going to do nothing, just like I thought.

"So what are you going to do?"

"Nothing. Learn how to crochet, maybe."

"We could use some doilies."

"Tracy, if you tell me to drop this investigation, then that's the final word."

"No it won't be, you big goof. You'll get grouchy, and you won't talk about anything else." She leaned over and picked up Mayhew, who was trying to climb my leg, and snuggled him against her neck. "Go ahead and keep on snooping. I don't mind. But if more work comes along, you'll have to drop this case."

"Of course."

"But who's going to help you? That Ambrose

Hatfield knows all the folks in his area, but who else does? I mean, somebody who'd help you?"

I thought of Bethany.

"Maybe the sister." I said.

"The one who makes Mamie Van Doren look like Mickey Rooney?"

"I never said that about her."

"I could hear it in your voice the first time you mentioned her. Is she married?" Mayhew let out a big squeak and Tracy put him back on the floor. He immediately swatted Eben who gave him a cuff back.

"Not anymore."

"Those divorcees are trouble."

"She's not exactly divorced. Listen, I just want to talk to her."

"Make sure you do just that."

"Can I call her now?"

"Can I listen in?" She smiled winningly.

I frowned "Only if you plug your ears."

I dialed Bethany's number.

"Hatfield residence," a little girl answered.

"Is your mom available?"

"Who may I say is calling?"

"Axe Hatchett."

"That's not a name."

"It is, too. Just give her that name."

"All right, but I hope this isn't one of those 'Prince Albert in a can' calls."

I waited. In a minute Bethany came on the line.

"Yes? Mister Hatchett?"

"Are you still talking to me?"

"Of course. Cuthbert's death wasn't your fault. And I'm sorry about the way Ambrose must have treated you."

"He fired me and he's not going to pay me. Granted, I didn't do a whole lot, but we had a contract."

"I'd let the matter go if I were you. Ambrose will drag you through every court in the state. That's how he is. He'll enjoy it."

"It doesn't matter. I want to keep investigating your brother's murder, and I'll do it on my own hook if I have to."

"Really? You aren't through? Why not let the police handle it?"

"Have they talked to you?"

No."

"I didn't think so. A little bird, with a badge, told me the cops are through with the case. They won't be doing anything more. It's me or nobody, but I need you to help me. Can you do that?"

"Of course."

"Do you spend enough time at your brothers' place to be familiar with their neighbors?"

"I know quite a few of them, yes. Mind you, none of them are friends of mine, but I know them through my brothers. I could give you some names."

"Swell."

"I'll do something else for you. I'll hire you back onto the case."

"You will? That'd be great. Do you think you could drop by my office and we can put together a contract?"

"Put together any kind of contract you want. I'll sign it."

"That's awfully trusting of you."

"Not really. You just told me you'd work to find my brother's murderer for free. What more do I need to know about you? I want you working for me, and I want to know exactly what's going on at all times."

"No problem. That's your right as a client. Could you put together a list of those neighbors?'

"I can. I'll do it tonight. I can't tell you exactly where they all live, but I can draw you a map."

Another damned map.

"That'd be good. It will give me a start. I'm going to have to rent or borrow a truck, or a Jeep."

"What about the truck you were driving the other day? The maroon one?"

"It belongs to my landlord. He's a great guy, but I hate to impose."

"Why don't you borrow my truck?"

"You'd let me do that?"

"Of course."

"I'll loan you my Chevy."

"You don't have to. I own a car, a Lincoln. I only use the truck when I drive up to Ambrose and Cuthbert's" Her divine voice cracked a little. "Or, just Ambrose now, I guess. I don't like driving it. Why don't I drop by your place tomorrow morning? I'll bring the truck and I can sign whatever contract you've put together. Then you can drive me back home."

"That'd be terrific. What time do you want to come over?"

"I've got to get my girls to school. How does nine sound?"

"Perfect. Let's hope it doesn't start snowing again. Could be none of us will be driving anywhere."

"True. I'll see you in the morning."

"Swell. Good bye."

Tracy had gone into the bedroom to give me privacy, but I think she'd been listening in. When I went into the bedroom, she had a big smile on her face.

"I'm working again," I told her.

"Congratulations! Did that Bethany broad hire you?"

"She did."

"And you'll be working with her really closely?"

"Not so much. Come on, Tracy, you know you're my only girl."

"It better stay that way. Come to bed."

"It's too early to go to sleep."

"Who said anything about sleeping?"

The next morning, at a little past nine, Bethany's truck pulled up in front of the building. I'd given her the address the night before. She came into my office wearing her fur-collared coat and a jaunty knit cap. I'd hardly helped her sit down in my client's chair when Tracy poked her head in the door. She was wearing her apron and cap and had mustard on her left hand.

"I hate to interrupt you," she told me. "I just wanted to know what kind of sandwich you wanted for lunch."

"Huh? Lunch is three hours away."

"Well, think about it anyway." She turned to face Bethany. "I'm Mrs. Hatchett," she said. She stuck out her left hand to shake Bethany's. Tracy is right-handed. She left a mustard smear on Bethany's nice lavender glove.

"Mrs. Hatfield," said Bethany.

"I thought that was your maiden name," said Tracy, giving her the eye.

"It was. I'm a widow."

"Oh? I'm sorry."

"I'm not. I shot the bastard."

Tracy, of all people, was taken aback.

"Oh. I guess that's one way to get rid of a bad husband. Did he cheat on you?" She gave me a meaningful glare.

Bethany laughed, little silver bells in sunlight. "Men don't cheat on me, darling."

"Well, it was nice meeting you. I got to get back to work." She turned to me. "Think about that sandwich."

When Tracy was gone Bethany removed her gloves and threw them in the trash. It must be nice to have that kind of money.

"I like her," she said. "Spunky. She'd be pretty if she didn't squint so."

"She won't wear her damned glasses."

"How unfortunate. She can't get a good look at her husband, or her supposed rivals. Shall we get down to business?"

"Let's."

I handed her the contract I'd drawn up and she signed it without even looking at it.

"I like you," she said. "I'm not entirely sure why I trust you so, but I do. I brought that list of names, and a map. Good luck finding some of these people. I think most of them hate Ambrose, and some of them hated Cuthbert, no doubt. Find which one of them arranged for my brother's death. I'll give you a bonus if you find out soon."

"I'll do my best, believe me."

"I can hardly convince myself he's really dead. The funeral's later this morning. I won't tell Ambrose I hired you." She stood up. "I hate to run, but I have to change into black. Could you drive me home?"

"Are your girls going to the funeral?"

"No. I didn't think that was a good idea."

I drove her home in her Dodge pickup. It ran swell. Bethany's house was in one of the pricier neighborhoods. I wondered how much money the Hatfield's had actually made from the sale of their granddaddy's land.

"What did your husband do for a living?" I asked, pulling up to the curb. I got out and went around and opened the door for her.

"He was a loan shark. That's not what he called himself, but that's what he was. He left me quite a bit of money. Of course, I also have money from the land my brothers and I sold. I guess I'm quite a catch, Mr. Hatchett. But men don't really care how much money a woman has, do they? They're more interested in looks."

"I suppose that's true. I'll keep in touch with you, Miss Hatfield."

"Bethany."

"Sure. And you should start calling me Axe."

"Good bye, Axe. Good luck."

I watched her walk to her door. A woman like her could give a man a whole lot of trouble, but I wasn't in the race anymore. I drove home and went into Ben and Allie's.

"Two egg sandwiches with cheese and onion," I told Tracy. "For my lunch. Now you don't have to worry about it anymore."

"She's not such a looker," she said.

I said nothing.

"She isn't," Tracy insisted.

"I didn't really notice," I said. "Listen, I've got to get to work."

"You aren't driving up to the Hatfield place, are you?"

"Nearby to them. Yes."

"Do you think the roads will be decent?"

"I hope they've plowed them by now. And there hasn't been any new snow."

"Watch out for that bear."

"I've got my shotgun loaded with double-ought buckshot. And I've got Ben's hog leg. Maybe we'll have bear for supper."

"We could make sandwiches out of it for days."

Ben spoke from behind the counter.

"No sandwiches from bears," he said. "The customers wouldn't like."

I kissed Tracy, and rubbed her cheek with my hand. "You're the only looker I'm interested in. Quit being so green-eyed."

"My eyes are brown."

"Like a doe's. Keep them that way."

11

I went back to my office. I looked over the map Bethany had prepared. There were half a dozen names on it, written next to where their houses were supposed to be. I figured I was in for some fun getting lost. I'd already talked to some of the people, but there were plenty of folks the Hatfield brothers hadn't mentioned to me.

I decided to get going. The sooner I made it to Flinders Cone, the sooner I'd have somebody to chat with. I put my shotgun and a flashlight in the cab of Bethany's truck, then ducked my head into the sandwich shop again.

"Could I have those sandwiches to go, Tracy?"

"You leaving already?"

"We'll have your sandwiches in a jiffy," said Ben.

"Make a couple of extra, could you? I don't know when I'm going to be back, and there aren't any restaurants up there."

"Sure," said Ben. "Four egg sandwiches?"

"Please, and thanks. Tracy will pay you for them."

"I'll work them off," she said.

"Find who this poor man was killed by," said Allie. She was busy waiting on customers.

"I'll do my level best."

I took my food, plus a thermos of coffee, kissed Tracy good bye, and climbed into the truck. The roads in town were plowed and sanded, but once I got up near Flinders Cone, things got rough. The main road, the one that bordered the Hatfield's lake, had been plowed some, but the side roads were still covered with snow. The only thing that made them bearable to drive on were the tracks made by other vehicles' tires.

I went up past Harvey Rundell's house. I hadn't yet talked to anyone who lived beyond that point. The first mailbox I came to proclaimed the property's owner to be Jister. Bethany had written the names Walter and Irene Jister on the map.

I pulled into a side road that could hardly be seen, it was so covered with snow. A quarter mile farther, I came in sight of a boxy cottage put together with native rock. I parked in front and sat a couple of minutes, then I got out and headed for the front porch.

A couple of harmless-looking pooches crawled out from under the porch and practiced their barking on me. They were getting pretty good at it. I knocked at a door that needed paint. A woman answered. She was slatternly, past middle age, red-headed, with freckles on her face and liver spots on her hands.

"There's a sign on the gatepost says no peddlers," she told me.

"I didn't see a gate post, and I'm not a peddler. My name's Axe Hatchett. I'm a private investigator. Can I take a moment of your time?"

"Walter ain't to home. He run to town."

"Well, I'd be happy to talk to you."

"I don't like letting people in when Walter's away."

"It's awfully cold standing on this porch. I can show you some identification."

"What's this about, young man?"

Thirty-six isn't young, but I guess she was old enough to think so.

"You no doubt have heard about your neighbor, Cuthbert Hatfield, getting killed by a bear the other day."

"Word gets around. Horrible!"

"Yes, it was. Have you by any chance seen the bear that attacked him?"

"How would I know which bear it was? Come on in. It's cold."

She let me inside. The house smelled like greasy meat, pipe tobacco, dirty laundry, Old Spice aftershave, dogs, and I don't know what all.

"Take a chair."

I selected one covered in fake leather with the cushion split. Mrs. Jister sat down on a matching couch. I described the Reaper to her.

"Never saw a bear like that in my life," she said. "Don't want to, neither. Why don't they shoot the thing?"

"I think they're trying to, but the bear's smart, and might be trained."

"You mean like a dancing bear?"

"More like a killing bear. It may have been trained to kill the Hatfields."

"No. You're funning me! Ain't no such a bear."

"I'm afraid he actually exists. I saw him myself. I'd like to find out who's keeping him."

"You mean he has a home?"

"Yes. I think he has a place where he can hole up. Do you know anyone who dislikes the Hatfields enough to want them dead?"

"Half the county, I'd say. That Cuthbert wrecked our Jeep. Run into it like a fool. He was driving too fast. Ran right into us when we was going the other way. Weren't nobody around to see the wreck, and he wouldn't take the blame for it. Didn't get a dime out of him."

"Really? That surprises me. I thought Cuthbert was the better brother."

"Better, maybe, but not good."

"You wouldn't have killed him for that though?"

"'Course I wouldn't. Are you crazy?"

"Who would have killed him?"

"I don't know. Why should I tell you? It ain't my business and I don't mourn Cuthbert any." She lit up a bent cigarette and coughed into her hand a couple of times.

"Well, here's how it is," I said. "I've dealt with a few murderers in my line of work."

"Really?"

"Yes. Sometimes they kind of develop a taste for killing. One murder isn't always enough for them. You don't want someone running around here killing folks right and left, do you?"

"With a bear?"

"Maybe he'll use a different weapon next time. A gun, or poison. Maybe he'll creep into your house some night and slit your throat while you're sleeping. You and your husband."

"Lord of mercy. You think?"

"I do. Now, who do you know around here who might have murderous intentions?"

"Maybe Elmer Katz. He's an odd one. A couple of years ago his wife run off with Ambrose Hatfield. Moved right in with both brothers. Ambrose brought her back after a time, just kind of dumped her on Elmer's porch. She's run off since then with others. I've heard Elmer curse a blue streak talking about the Hatfields."

"What does Mr. Katz do for a living?"

"Works in a coal mine. Coughs a lot, but he's tough."

"Is he good with animals?"

"Couldn't train up a bear to kill folks, if that's what you mean. Couldn't train a chicken to peck."

"Do the Katz's live near you?"

"Up the road. But Elmer's likely at work. Adelaide might be home, if she hasn't run off with somebody else."

"Just up the road? Your side of the road?"

"Sure. The Hatfields own all the land on the other side of the road. You ought to know that."

"You're right. Well, thank you for your time, Mrs. Jister. I'll be going now."

"You see that bear, you fill its hide full of buckshot for us."

"I'll do just that. I came prepared."

I drove on up the road until a wobbly mailbox proclaimed that I had reached the Katz abode. The house was made of logs with a frame addition on one side that looked like it'd been built about the time Orville and Wilber were playing with paper airplanes. I parked and headed for the house.

No dogs greeted me. No one answered my knock either. I looked around. There was a kind of low-roofed barn on one side. It wasn't locked. There was nothing inside but an ancient Pontiac and some tools and trash.

I walked around the lot. I found tracks. Big bear tracks. They came out of the forest, circled around in the clearing, and led back into the woods.

Just to be doing something I took the dog whistle out of my pocket and blew on it and waited. I blew on it again. Nothing happened. I got back in the truck and drove on down the road.

The next mailbox said: "Royster." I drove down the half-mile long drive. The Roysters lived in a fairly modern frame house the color of a fish belly.

Three dogs appeared and investigated the truck. I got out slowly and the dogs barked, but backed off. I went to the front door and rang the bell. There was no response. I tried again, without success, and then took a look around.

Behind the house was a big barn, and between it and the house was a man exercising a horse. There was a long lead rope attached to the bridle. The man, a tall fellow, was holding the other end of the lead rope and was making the horse walk in a circle around him. I couldn't imagine why.

"Mr. Royster?" I called. He jumped no more than the height of the horse, a spotted one, and turned around.

"Didn't hear you," he said. He was smiling.

I went over and introduced myself, keeping an eye on the horse. I didn't want to get trampled.

"What can I do for you?" the man asked. He hadn't given me his name.

"I'm investigating the death of Cuthbert Hatfield. He's the man who was killed by a bear a few days ago."

"I know. Hope that bear doesn't come around here. You a forest ranger?"

"No. Private investigator."

"Oh? Like a detective?"

"The same."

"You want to talk about that bear?"

"Have you seen it?"

"Oh, yes, I have. I talked to Cuthbert about it the other week and he described it to me. Last night, the dogs started barking and carrying on. And then old Dapple here started making a fuss in the barn. We could hear him all the way in the house. I grabbed my rifle and went out with a flashlight to see what's what.

"This bear walked right into my light. Big as a house. Blondie-brown. Hump on his back. Liked to have scared me to death. I shot my rifle in the air and he run off."

"Why didn't you shoot the bear?"

"Thought I might just wound him, and then he'd come and kill me."

"Was there anything unusual about the bear's behavior?"

"What do you mean? What's usual about a bear? They're all crazy, if you ask me. Never did like them."

"I don't know. Did he act like he was used to being around people? Was he afraid of your gun, before you fired it?"

I made the mistake of stepping too close to the horse. It snorted and began prancing around, pulling at its lead rope. I jumped back quick enough.

"You'll have to excuse Dapple. He's a bit skittish. He belongs to a neighbor of mine. He wants me to teach it some manners, but the last couple of months or so I just haven't had the time." He patted the horse and spoke to it, calming it a little. Dapple snorted and rolled his eyes.

"I've been trying different bits on him to see if I can find one he'll pay attention to. He's got a hard mouth. Maybe I should just put him back in the barn."

"Fine by me."

I followed Royster into the big barn while he led the horse.

"Did you say the bear was scared of you?"

"Didn't seem to be. I don't know. I was scared of the bear. Does that count?"

We were in the barn now. Royster led Dapple over to a stall and got him settled. There was a second stall. As I was passing it, I noticed something. A tuft of yellow-brown fur, stuck in a splintered post.

While the man's back was turned I nabbed the piece of fur and slipped it into my pocket. Jackpot. At least I hoped so.

"What do you do for a living, Mr. Royster?"

"I'm a roofer. But that's mostly in the summer. Winters I do a little of this and that."

"That seems to be a popular occupation up here."

"Roofing?"

"No. A little of this and that."

He laughed. "I guess that's so."

We left the barn. I noticed a green panel truck parked nearby.

"What do you do with that?" I asked.

"Oh, drive it. Haul stuff. I wasn't really looking for a panel, but I got it for a good price. It comes in handy."

I bet it does, I thought.

"Let me ask you another question. Have you got any particular beef with the Hatfields?"

"No. I kind of liked Cuthbert. I've heard some things against Ambrose, but I haven't had any trouble with him. Out here, in the mountains, it pays to get along with your neighbors. You never know when you might need their help."

While we were walking back toward the house, I looked for bear tracks. I didn't see any.

"I hate to take up any more of your time, Mr. Royster. I just wanted to know if you'd seen that bear."

"Well, like I said, I have. And I don't want to see him again. Next time the dogs and the horse start acting up at night, I might just stay in the house."

When we got close to my truck, the dogs gathered round again. They started growling in earnest and moving in my direction.

"None of that," Royster told them, and they settled right down and grew quiet.

I thanked Royster again and got into Bethany's truck. I was feeling pretty good.

I noticed that another storm was moving in. I couldn't see the top of Finders Cone, even though it was only a few miles away. The snow would be coming down soon, and I didn't want to get stuck in the mountains — where would I stay? Certainly not with Ambrose.

I decided to head back to town. I had some stuff to think about. And it was time to talk to Bethany again. I wondered if she knew of any grudge Mr. Royster might have with her brothers.

It started snowing again before I got back home, and the going was real slow. I ate two of my sandwiches while I crawled back to town. Before long, even in town, it was practically a blizzard. I parked the truck and went into the sandwich shop. Tracy, Ben, and Allie were all there, but they didn't have much to do. The storm was keeping customers away.

"Any luck?" Tracy asked me.

"I'll say." I showed her the tuft of bear fur.

"Pretty. Where's the rest of the bear?"

"Roaming the woods. I think his trainer has abandoned him now that he's done his job. Either that, or he's still working, trying to finish the job by killing Ambrose."

I told her the rest of what I knew. The bear tracks, Royster's working with the horse, my finding the tuft of fur in one of Royster's barn stalls.

"He wouldn't have that horse at his place if the bear was still boarding in his barn," I said. "If we're lucky, Cuthbert was the only intended murder victim. I need to talk to Bethany again."

"Don't invite her over."

"Why? I thought you said she wasn't that much of a looker"

"I wasn't wearing my glasses."

"You never wear them. I'm surprised you don't make sandwiches with the filling on the outside."

"I want contacts."

"Nonsense. They're bad for people's eyes. They'd make you cross-eyed, and you're funny-looking enough already. Besides, we can't afford them."

"I look like a spinster fish monger when I wear glasses."

"I've known some pretty classy-looking fish mongers."

"No you haven't. Why don't you go upstairs and play with the kittens? Ben and Allie are thinking of closing early. We don't have any business, and they want to get home before the roads get worse. I'll join you when I can."

"Trying to get rid of me?"

"No, but I can tell that cork skull of yours is full of ideas. Go call your dreamboat. Talk to her about the horse guy."

"I guess I will."

I went outside again and up the stairs to our apartment. The kittens came out of nowhere and wound themselves around my legs.

"Do you guys know anything about bears?" I asked them. They didn't. I let the sniff the tuft of bear fur. They like it. I had to snatch it away from them before they ate it. Hooligans.

I called Bethany. If she was home, she didn't answer the phone. That left me with just my thoughts. Had Cuthbert been murdered by committee? Hop as the bear trainer, Royster as the guy who hid the bear, and some unknown person paying them to have the Reaper kill Cuthbert and

Ambrose?

If you're interested in killing someone, it's best to do the work yourself and not drag other people into it. They might squawk, and then you're sunk. However, sometimes murderers don't have a choice. I ate another sandwich.

12

I was tired of toting Ben's big forty-five around. I put it on the nightstand in our bedroom, in case the kittens needed protection, and grabbed my spare thirty-eight from the nightstand drawer. Ben still had my other revolver. Then I tried the phone again. This time Bethany answered.

"You been out in this weather?" I asked her.

"Yes, doing some shopping. I came home early. It's getting bad out there. Have you returned from the mountains?"

"Yes. Let me ask you something I just thought of. Why does Cuthbert's ex-wife work as a factory girl? I got the impression that both the ex-wives were pretty well fixed with alimony and child support."

"True. But Melinda's obsessed with the idea of supporting her kids with her own money. It's a matter of pride. She doesn't like the idea of needing her ex-husband's help. On top of that, she's saving as much money as possible for her kids' futures. She wants them to go to college. The best schools possible. She wants her boys to be the best that they can be."

"I see. What do you know about a Mr. Royster?"

"Whip Royster? Well — "

"Whip?"

"He trains horses. That's how he got the name, I guess. I don't know much about him. Melinda dated him for a time."

"That's interesting. So the guy's not married?"

"No. I think he's considered quite a catch. He's handsome. He can be quite charming. And he appears to have some money, though he doesn't like to spend it. Melinda says he's as cheap as a stingy hobo. I don't know where his money came from, or if he actually has any. I think he works as a roofer. Why are you asking about him?"

"He's been keeping a bear in his barn. I figure he and Hop Carlson might be working together."

"You think the Reaper belongs to them?"

"That's what I figure. Do you happen to know if Whip Royster hates Ambrose, or hated Cuthbert?"

"I'm sure he was annoyed with Cuthbert. As I said, Melinda dated Whip, and Cuthbert did everything he could to get in their way. He told Whip all kinds of bad things about Melinda, none of them true. And he had plenty of bad tales to tell Melinda about Whip.

"Not only that, but he followed them around.

They'd go out on a date, and damned if Cuthbert wouldn't show up. He tried picking fights with Whip. He may even have let the air out of Whip's truck tires. He was pretty childish."

"Sounds like it. I take it that Melinda and Whip aren't dating anymore. Do you think Cuthbert succeeded in breaking them up?"

"I really couldn't say."

"I may want to talk to Melinda again, but she's hard to get ahold of, and I don't think she likes me. Is she your friend?"

"Not like with me and Kelly, but we're friends, yes. Do you want me to set up a lunch date for the three of us? I mean, Melinda and me and you?"

"That'd be swell. Could you pick a place other than the Gypsy Wagon? I'd kind of like to fill my belly this time."

"Oh, don't worry, Melinda will give you a belly full. If you thought Kelly was full of acid, wait until you meet Melinda."

"Gee, I'm really looking forward to it."

She laughed. Violins and orchids. "I'll see if I can set something up. It could be tough. She only gets a half hour for lunch when she's working, and she spends as much time as she can with her kids when she's off. Dinner might be better than lunch."

"That works fine for me."

"OK. I'll let you know if I get something set up. Talk to you later. Keep working on the case."

"It's all I think about. Let me ask you one thing

more. You've talked to Ambrose since I have. Did he give you the whole story about how your brother was killed? I mean, I hate to ask for details, but I need to know."

"It was pretty awful. I guess the bear came up from behind them. They didn't even hear it. It attacked Ambrose and knocked him down. Cuthbert wasn't carrying a gun, so he jumped on the Reaper's back. The bear shook him off and tore out his throat." Her voice got teary for a moment.

"Ambrose only had time to get off one shot before the bear ran back into the woods."

"That's terrible! So Cuthbert died trying to save his brother's life. That must make Ambrose feel even worse."

"Yes, if he's still capable of having decent feelings. Last time I talked to Ambrose he was cursing Cuthbert for being such a fool. He shouldn't have jumped on the Reaper's back."

"He's upset, that's all. He's all bent out of shape."

"He ought to be."

"Well, thanks for talking to me. Let me know when you get our date set up."

I hung up.

Now I had more things to think about. If Cuthbert was the one who'd had the bear trained, perhaps the reality of seeing his brother get mauled had changed his mind, and so he'd tried to stop it from happening. The bear, now full of blood lust, might have turned on Cuthbert and killed him without even thinking about it.

Since the bear attacked Ambrose first, it now seemed doubtful that Ambrose had been using the bear to kill his brother.

What Bethany had told me about Whip was also interesting. If he'd been serious about dating Cuthbert's ex-wife, then getting rid of Cuthbert made sense. Also, if both the brothers were killed, then Melinda's sons would inherit enough money to get gold-plated bicycles and baseball bats. Since their mom would be in charge of the money until the boys grew up, Whip would have a lot of loose change to invest if Melinda cooperated.

Tracy came upstairs after another hour.

"Shop's closed," she said. She had a big stack of sandwiches with her. "The cats might have to help us with these."

"Over my dead body."

"Maybe. They're pretty tough. We had some leftover sandwich fillings today, so I put together some kind of unusual sandwiches. Peanut butter and turkey breast. Deviled ham and tuna salad on rye. Cream cheese and corned beef with pickle relish. You're going to love them. Did you talk to your little movie idol?"

"I did. She's arranging a date with me. But her former sister-in-law's coming."

"Can I come, too?"

"No. You're a lousy operative." Tracy had helped me a little with an earlier case and had almost ruined things.

"I need practice, that's all. Come on. Let me make it a quartet."

"Not this time, angel. I've got to go it alone."

"Poor long-suffering you."

The next couple of days passed very slowly. The snow stopped, but there was no real point in my going back to the mountains yet. I needed to talk to Melinda first. Finally, Bethany called me.

"How's seven o'clock this evening sound? At the Blue Ox? You're paying. I've already made reservations."

"If I'm paying for dinner, then I'm including it in my expenses for the Hatfield Bear Case. That means you'll be paying for it."

"Fine by me. Melinda's the one who insisted she not have to pay."

"I'll be looking forward to it. What should I wear for my meeting with Melinda? Armor?"

"Wouldn't do you any good. She's got a mouth like a battering ram. You'll be OK. You're a tough guy. See you at seven?"

"Sure. Should I pick you up?"

"No, I'll pick you up. You're my date. Tell your near-sighted cutie I said, 'Hi.'"

"I'll do that."

When seven o'clock came near, I donned a swell hand-me-down suit a former client's butler had given me. In fact, one of our kittens, Mayhew, was named after the guy. Tracy looked me over with disapproval.

"You look too good to be going out with

swanky dames. Can't you muss up your hair or something?"

"I could break my nose again."

"I'll break it for you if you get home any later than nine."

"I'm on a case, remember?"

"Eat fast and don't talk any more than you have to. Eat with your mouth open and wipe it on your sleeve."

"I'll ruin the Blue Ox's reputation."

"No, just yours."

Bethany picked me up in a swell silver-gray Lincoln convertible with the top up.

"Well, Mr. Hatchett," she said, eyeing me up and down. "You look quite dashing."

"You look pretty OK yourself."

She was wearing a slinky burgundy dress with an ermine stole over it.

"Just OK?"

"That's as much as a married man would dare say."

"I know some married men who'd say a lot more. But you're a newlywed."

I'd met plenty of dames like Bethany. Lookers who knew exactly what they had and what it could get them. They played with men the way they'd once played with their dolls and their cute Scotty dogs. But it seldom meant anything.

The Blue Ox was a champion steak house. I couldn't have picked a better place, especially since my new client was picking up the tab. We arrived before Melinda and were steered to a table near a roaring fire place. Bethany ordered a cocktail, a gin fizz, and I had my usual coffee.

"Afraid of losing your self-control?" she asked me.

"No. But I consider this part of my work. I don't drink on the job."

"You're so conscientious."

In a few minutes we were joined by a knockout in a brown suit. The suit was nothing special, but Melinda was. She had a lot of reddish-blonde hair, two very long legs, an upturned nose and a dimpled chin. Eyes like amber coals. She looked surprisingly sweet considering Bethany's description of her personality.

"I'm late. I'm sorry," Melinda said in a tiny voice as smooth as oil in a Rolls Royce's crankcase.

"We just got here," Bethany allowed. "I'm still on my first drink."

I pulled out a chair for the new arrival and got a whiff of drugstore perfume. She really was saving her money for her boys.

"I'm Axe Hatchett. Private investigator. We talked on the phone."

"Yes. I'm sorry if I was short with you. I was busy. I don't have much time for motel peepers, especially the kind my ex-husband would hire."

"Sure. But I wouldn't exactly describe myself as a motel peeper."

"Call yourself whatever you want. I know what you are. You slimy gum heels are all alike. I hired one of you guys once to follow Cuthbert. All I got for my money was a leer and some lies."

"Yeah. I don't care much for my competition either. You should have hired me. Maybe you still will someday.

"Don't hold your breath unless you're a pearl diver."

Our waiter came over, took Melinda's drink order — a double brandy Alexander — and promised to bring Bethany another gin fizz.

"I'm sorry about your ex-husband's death," I said.

"I didn't want him dead. Not really. But you'll excuse me if I'm not entirely grief-stricken. I just wish it'd been Ambrose instead. From what Bethany has told me, Ambrose is the one who should be dead. If only Cuthy hadn't been so brave. That must have been the first time in his life he ever showed courage. Unless he was a war hero. I wouldn't know. He never talked about it. He bored me with other stories."

We drank our drinks and then ordered dinner. I picked out a lovely T-bone off the menu, with mashed potatoes and gravy. The girls ordered smaller steaks.

"Axe is working for me now," Bethany told Melinda. It was the second time she'd called me by my first name.

Melinda frowned. "Mr. Hatchett doesn't appear to be a very fast worker," She lifted an elegant eyebrow. "At least not when it comes to investigating. Maybe he could have prevented Cuthy's death."

"I did my best," I said, "but things happened pretty fast. I don't know why Ambrose couldn't kill the bear with it almost on top of him. He claims to be a great hunter, and I've seen him shoot. If he's as good with a rifle as he is with a revolver, that bear should have died some time ago."

"Ambrose claims to have shot it twice," said Bethany.

I shook my head. "I was with him for one of those shots. At night. He said his bullet hit a tree branch."

"When Cuthbert was killed," said Bethany, "Ambrose said he put a bullet in the Reaper's shoulder as he was running away."

"Ambrose always was a bragger," said Melinda. "Maybe he's not such a crack shot when there's danger involved."

"I think I've asked you this before," I said to Melinda. "Do you know of anybody who would want Cuthbert dead? Or Ambrose, for that matter. Who would hate the brothers that much? Or who would benefit from their deaths the most?"

"My sons will benefit from their father's death. All his money and property will now belong to them. Of course, I'll have control of everything until they're twenty-one. It takes a load off my mind. I always had to treat Cuthbert better than I wanted to. I was afraid he'd get mad and change his will.

But, actually, I don't think he ever would have. He loved his sons too much. It's good to know that he was actually capable of loving someone."

"Looks like he was pretty attached to his brother. He died for him."

"Sure. They were close. Surrounded by all the people who hated them, who else did they have?"

"But you haven't named anyone specifically who would want them dead. I mean, is there someone who'd actually be willing to kill them?"

"I don't know any murderers, no."

"I gather that only one of the brothers had to die for your sons to inherit, rather than both." I turned to Bethany. "Was the property already split up between the three of you?"

Bethany had finished her second drink and was looking around for our waiter. "When our granddaddy died, he left everything to me, Ambrose, and Cuthbert. But, to answer your question, yes. Everything was split into thirds, both the money and the land. When Ambrose and Cuthbert decided to sell some of their land, I allowed them to sell some of mine as well. Now that Cuthbert is dead, Ambrose can't stand in the way of his nephews getting everything Granddaddy left Cuthbert."

"I see," I said. "So if Ambrose dies, only his two boys will benefit."

"Yes, although Kelly will be in charge of the money for a while. However, both of my brothers made it hard for any of the money to be spent on anything but their boys."

I turned to Melinda.

"I hear that you and Whip Royster were boy and girl for a time. Did Cuthbert cause enough trouble to break you up?"

"I wouldn't give him that much satisfaction. I wasn't very serious about Whip. I doubt if I'll ever be serious about a man again. Don't get any ideas about Whip killing Cuthbert. He could train a bear, but he's not a murderer, just a spineless creep."

"I understood that he trains horses. That doesn't mean he can handle a bear."

"Sure he could. He used to work with Hop Carlson training wild animals. Haven't your clever investigations turned up Hop yet?"

"Yes. Did Hop and Whip both work for that little family zoo down in Louisiana?"

"Yes, but something happened. An animal killed a pair of three-year-old twins. Hop and Whip had trained the beast, whatever it was. I think it was a cougar. They were both fired because of it. Hop gave up animal training and moved out here, but they stayed friends. A couple of years ago, Whip moved out here, too. He became a horse trainer. And a roofer. Since then, I think he's come into some money, but he'll never have enough."

Our steaks arrived. We ate them, but I forgot to chew with my mouth open, and I used my napkin.

Nothing much more happened during the dinner, and Melinda wasn't anything like the monster

Bethany had represented her to be. Maybe I just didn't know her well enough: she might save her worst behavior for those who are closest to her.

When Bethany dropped me off home, she idled her Lincoln in front of my place for a couple of minutes.

"What did you think of Melinda?"

"I was disappointed. She wasn't the fire-breather you claimed she was. I liked my steak, though."

"Well, that's what counts. What would your little wife do if you came home with my very red lipstick on your collar?"

"I'm not going to find out."

"No?" She leaned across the seat and quickly kissed me. She missed my collar.

"I don't let my clients kiss me," I told her.

"You're turning a very nice shade of red," she replied, though how she could tell in the light from the dash, I can't imagine.

"Don't ever do that again," I said.

I got out of the car and slammed its expensive door. I could still hear Bethany laughing. For once it wasn't a pleasant sound. I went into the house, scrubbing at my mouth with my show hanky. I felt like a sweet little cheerleader who's fullback date just got too fresh. Tracy would love this.

13

"What's you got on your lips," she demanded, as soon as I walked into our little living room. Even the kittens looked suspicious.

"Nothing. Steak sauce," I lied. "Listen, Tracy, angel, it's not what you think. The damned dame threw herself at me. And not because I'm Tyrone Power. She's trouble. She likes playing dangerous games."

"I'll kill her. Maybe you too. I want you off of this case." Her face was screwed up into a knot and her eyes blazed pure lava.

"We need the money. And there's a murderer loose somewhere."

"Give me that Bethany dame's address. I'm going to pay her a little visit."

"Don't. Please. I'll drop the case."

"Give me her address or I'll look it up myself. Let me get my car keys."

I couldn't stop her.

"Let me go with you," I said. "Bethany can't

even be home yet."

I still had my coat on. Tracy grabbed hers.

"You can take me to her place, but you have to stay in the car," she told me.

We headed down the stairs together. I opened the door and we stepped outside. I'd just put my hat back on my head, when somebody across the street shot it off.

I grabbed Tracy and swung her around behind me. A second shot just grazed my neck and chipped a brick in the wall behind us.

I pulled my thirty-eight from my overcoat pocket and returned fire. I didn't dare hunker down and expose Tracy. I fired twice, aiming at the shop straight across from us. I heard my bullets smack into brick.

Someone moved and ran low along the sidewalk and ducked into an alley. I sent another bullet at the gunman and then turned to Tracy. "Get inside! Now!" I waited until she was inside the door and then gave chase.

The alley was as dark as old sin. I couldn't see a damned thing, but I could hear running footsteps. I followed. At the end of the alley I came out onto a street. The streetlight showed me nothing.

I heard a car start up and headed in that direction. Headlights hit me in the face and I ducked down. The vehicle roared past me, but there were no more shots. I turned to look at it, maybe get the license number, but my eyes had been blinded by the headlights. I couldn't see a damned thing.

There was nothing more for me to do. I ran back down the alley and met Tracy half-way along it. She threw herself into my arms.

"You all right?" she shouted, though her mouth was practically against my ear.

I winced. "Right as rain. And you?"

"I'm fine. I called the cops. You're not shot?"

"Not so you'd notice."

I saw in the light of the street lamp that she was clutching the big revolver of Ben's. I'd left it on the nightstand in our bedroom.

"No more gun play tonight." I said.

"Oh, I don't know. I've got two people to kill now. That brassy dame, and the guy that shot at you."

"That's my girl." I gave her a squeeze until she squeaked.

I took her inside. The kittens mewed and looked as us expectantly.

"I guess you guys somehow think you deserve treats," I told them, and fetched their sack of tuna jerky.

The cops arrived in a few minutes, and damned if I didn't know one of them. Officer Biff Munson. As a cop, he'd been involved in a couple of cases of mine.

"Jeez, Axe, couldn't you pick a nicer night to get shot at?" he greeted me.

"Sorry. It's awfully damned inconsiderate of me."

His partner was a little guy with a very serious

151

face. He took a notebook from his pocket. I knew he'd have to make a damned police report, and who knew how long we'd be kept up past our bedtime.

Tracy was dabbing iodine, or something equally obnoxious, on my neck wound. But it was nothing but a scratch. My hat was worse off. It had a nice little hole through the crown. And it was only three years old!

"My husband could have been killed!" Tracy told the officers, like it was somehow their fault.

"And what about you?" I asked Tracy, burning at the thought of her getting hurt. "Chasing after me and the gunman with Ben's six-shooter. You could have been killed, too, you monkey!"

Biff got a big goofy grin on his face and took off his hat. He's not even half as stupid as he looks.

"Are you Mrs. Hatchett?" he asked her.

"I sure am."

Biff turned to me. "You're a cradle robber, brother, but you got yourself one tough dame. Congratulations! Me and Marge, we got hitched, too. What do you think?"

"This calls for a cigar," I said. "Let me fetch a couple." I untangled myself from Florence Nightingale and found the partly-empty box of cigars Tracy's mom and pop had given me for Christmas.

"You got a little something to wet it down?" asked Biff, licking his lips.

"I'm afraid not," I said, and I felt genuinely bad.

"That's OK," he said, "I got a bottle in the squad car we took off a drunk." He turned toward his partner. "Millhousey, fetch that bottle, will you?"

"We're on duty," the little guy complained.

"We got a double wedding to celebrate. Get the bottle. You don't have to drink none."

"It's evidence," Millhousey said.

"Won't be for long," said Biff.

The little guy went out reluctantly to the black-and-white.

"He's new," Biff said. "He hasn't learned how to break the rules yet. Tell me what happened here."

"Guy shot at us. Or, at me. Tracy and me had just stepped out the door. There's a little light over it. Guy shot from across the street. He couldn't have seen much through the snow. I think he shot at my head.

"One slug went through my hat, damn it, and the other one grazed my neck, like you see. What kind of guy aims for the head, at forty feet, at night, in a snow storm?"

"You tell me. What kind of a guy?"

"Someone who thinks he knows how to shoot. I might know who it was. I'm not sure. I'm not even sure if it was his truck I saw."

"What's the guy's name?"

Millhousey returned with the hooch. It was the cheapest kind of whiskey you can get without shopping in an alley.

"This calls for glasses," Biff said.

Tracy rummaged around in our kitchen and came up with four jelly glasses. Biff filled them half-full and handed them around.

"Here's to wedded bliss," Biff said. We all drank except for Biff's partner. He set the glass on a lamp table and looked at it like it had done something illegal.

"Take down the report," Biff told him.

Millhousey brought out a notebook and licked the tip of a pencil.

I talked until I was through talking. It didn't take long. I gave the two cops Ambrose Hatfield's name, phone number, and address.

"He'll get away with it," Biff assured me. "I wonder if one of them slugs can be recovered in decent shape."

"I doubt it," I said. "They probably both hit the brick wall."

"I'll take a look," said Biff.

He unfolded a jack knife and went downstairs and outside. In a few minutes, he came back, poured another drink for three of us then drank down Millhousey's. He showed me a couple of flattened pieces of lead.

"Both in the wall," he said. "Big slugs. I'd say forty-fives. But they're mashed. Ballistics can't likely do nothing with them."

"Thanks for trying," I said. "If he'd hurt Tracy, I'd kill him."

"No more crimes," Biff warned me. "We got

our fill. Though, come to think of it, if some squirrel took a shot in Marge's direction I'd be blowing steam, too."

The stalwart constables left. Biff took the bottle with him.

"It's evidence, you know," he told us.

Tracy acted like I'd taken a broadside from a scatter-gun. She kept checking the bandage on my neck every minute or two. She insisted I get in bed and prop my feet up, though what that was supposed to do I couldn't guess.

"Now you have to drop the case," she told me.

"No. Now I have to solve it. I've been warned. I won't stick my head out the door again without a careful look around. I'll be all right."

"We don't need the money that bad. I'll get a second job."

"You'll do nothing of the kind. You can't baby me all the time. I can take care of myself."

"I see that."

I got up and paced around. I gave the cats more treats. Why the hell not?

"I didn't get shot up much, did I? I dodged those slugs just fine."

"Do what you want. Only don't make me a widow. I'm too young, and black's not my color."

"I'm going to make a couple of phone calls."

"Who you going to call?"

"Bethany, for one. Don't worry, she can's kiss me over the phone."

"If she coos in your ear, I'll pull the phone cord

out of the wall and strangle her with it."

"Fair enough."

I made the call. I got her bratty kid again.

"Hatfield residence."

"Let me speak to your mom."

"Who shall I say is calling?"

"Axe Hatchett, and it is too a name."

"Just a moment, Mr. Hatchett."

"Yes?" Bethany cooed. I shielded the earpiece with my hand and looked to see if Tracy was listening. She was pretending to be busy playing with our pets.

"Axe. Somebody took a couple of shots at me not long after you dropped me off."

"Oh, no! Are you all right?"

"Sure, I'm fine. But things are getting dicey. Who would want me off of this case?"

"The murderer, of course."

"And your brother. Do you happen to know where he was about eight-thirty?"

"No. At home, I assume. I haven't talked to him since early this afternoon. You think Ambrose took those shots at you? I don't. He's too good a shot. He would have killed you."

"The light was bad, and he was shooting through falling snow. He couldn't have seen me very well."

"I'm very sorry. Do you want off the case?"

"Not a chance. I've got both feet in it, and I'm not budging. Is Melinda home?"

"I'm sure she is. She's probably in bed by now.

Don't call and wake her. She didn't shoot at you. She hates guns, unlike me."

"I'm still putting my money on your brother as the shooter."

"Don't go anywhere near him."

"I might have to. If I need to talk to him, I'm not going to use the phone. He'd only hang up on me. Listen, I just wanted you to know what was going on. Good night."

"I'm sorry about what happened earlier. I was being a bitch. I'm not trying to take you away from your cutie. I just don't like mustard on my new gloves."

"I understand. But hands off. OK?"

"You got it, tough guy."

I hung up.

14

Who was Archie Pall? That was the question I had to ponder the next morning.

Tracy had pulled the mail out of our box yesterday afternoon. She'd left in on the coffee table, and we both forgot to look at it. I found it in the morning, and there was a letter from an Archie Pall, addressed to Ax Hatchet. Wrong spelling. Archie Pall hadn't looked me up in the phone book, he'd heard my name from someone.

Was it his real name? Probably. Most folks aren't good at aliases. They come up with names like John Smith or Jim Jones. Archie Pall sounded like the real thing.

He'd written me to ask that I give him a call, and he'd given a number that I guessed was a phone booth because he'd asked me to call him at five sharp. Of course, I didn't, because I hadn't seen the letter. Had he been the guy who'd taken a couple of shots at me? No way of knowing. He'd only heard my name, but he'd somehow known my address. I figured that somebody who had my business card had read my address to Archie over the phone, but they hadn't bothered to spell my name for him.

Who? Ambrose? Bethany? Cuthbert, before he was killed? It was driving me crazy. It had something to do with the bear. The note said: "This has something to do with the bear you're looking for." Swell.

I paced around the apartment all morning. I waited for the mail. I was hoping that when I hadn't called that maybe Archie had sent another letter. It could have made the morning mail, but it wasn't there when I checked.

At about noon, I heard the phone in my office ring downstairs. If it's quiet in the apartment, I can just barely hear it. I hurried downstairs, but by the time I got the door open, the phone had stopped ringing. I cursed. Then the phone in the apartment started ringing. I busted my hump getting upstairs to answer it.

"Axe Hatchett," I said, breathlessly.

"Mr. Hatchett? This is Archie Pall."

"Mr. Pall, I'm sorry I didn't call you. I didn't get your note until this morning. I tried calling then, but no one answered."

"It's a phone booth. Sorry. I don't have a phone. I tried calling a couple of days ago, but nobody answered. I guess we ain't having much luck with phones."

"I'm on the horn now," I said. "What do you

have to tell me? About the bear?"

"I know where it came from."

"Are you the owner?"

"No. Never was. But I know who owns it. If anybody can own a bear."

"And you're going to tell me?"

"I don't know if I am. I don't want to rat on a pal."

"Would the pal's name be Hop, or Whip?"

"Don't make guesses. That won't do you any good."

"What do you want? Money?"

"We all need money, but that's not why I'm calling. I just want to ease a guilty conscience. It wasn't me that trained that bear, but I was its keeper for a time."

"You sold it to someone else?"

"I gave it away. I was being sentimental. That bear has a history. There were some who wanted it put down."

"There's likely a whole lot of folks who want that right now. Keep talking, Mr. Pall. You haven't told me much yet."

He sighed.

"I guess I've got to give you the whole story, huh?"

"That'd be nice."

"That bear — his name is Gus — was a trained bear in a circus I worked in."

"Are you an animal trainer?"

"Me? No. I do the electrical stuff. Setting up all

the lights and such. But I always get to know the animals pretty well, wherever I'm working. I like them. This Gus, he was amazing. He was brought up with dogs, and so he acted like a dog. They even used him for hunting. He could track anything.

"The guy who owned him needed money, so he sold the bear to the circus. Gus was as smart as a whip, and a good bear. He never caused any trouble. But one day he just went kind of crazy. I think it was something he smelled. Maybe another bear. This circus didn't have any other bears — it was just Gus — and he'd never been around other bears, so the scent could have been a new one to him.

"We were up in the woods, not so far from Quartz Quarry, over in Wavering Haze. We'd set up our tents outside of town near the woods. Gus started pacing around in his cage, growling and chuffing and carrying on. His keeper tried to calm him down, and Gus went for him. He didn't kill him, just knocked him down and worried his arm a little. No harm done. The keeper was fine. But of course we had to report it to the circus owners."

"What's the name of this circus?"

"Jake and Zelda's Colossal Tent Circus. It's a five-and-dime kind of operation. The circus owners said we'd have to get rid of Gus. Sell him or put him down. Now, I ask you, who's going to buy a bear these days? We couldn't find a buyer, so we were going to shoot him. I couldn't stand that, so I offered to buy the bear myself.

"Of course, I don't have much money, and they wondered how I was going to keep the bear. I've got a station wagon, so I thought the bear could stay in that until I found a better place, but the circus folks, my bosses, said no. They were going to shoot him.

"I stole Gus that night. I just loaded him into my station wagon, and took off."

"What did you plan on doing with Gus?"

"Find a place for him. I had an idea. You see, years ago I worked for this little zoo where they trained some of their animals to do tricks. A real crowd pleaser."

"Was this in Louisiana?"

"Oh. You know that already? Yeah. The place was called Swampy's Wild Animal Paradise. They paid me and the trainers almost nothing, and they treated us worse than they treated their animals. I'm surprised they didn't throw hunks of meat at us at lunch time."

"So you worked with Hop Carlson and Whip Royster."

"You know a lot! Yeah, I worked with them. When the circus came to Wavering Haze, I looked them up. For old time's sake. When you work in my kind of business, you end up knowing a lot of folks, and you kind of keep track of them if they're friends.

"Hop, he wouldn't hardly speak to me. He told me that this part of his life was over and he just wanted to put it behind him. But Whip — he was happy to hear from me."

"And you told him you had a hot bear you needed to find a home for."

"That's right. Gee, I really feel bad about ratting on my pal."

"I don't think you have a choice, Mr. Pall. That bear just killed someone."

"Yeah, but that ain't my fault. I didn't raise Gus. I didn't train him."

"You stole him. You let him live. Listen, I can understand why a guy who likes animals would want to save Gus, but it wasn't good judgment."

"I'm going to be in trouble, right?"

"I figure. But at least you're owning up to what you did. You aren't going to be charged with murder or anything. You need to make things good with the circus people, tell them why you did what you did. And you need to go to the cops. Tell them the whole story. Tell them you gave Gus to Whip Royster, and you think he trained it up to kill a couple of guys. Whip's the one who's going to be in trouble."

"And I just ratted on him. You don't really think he trained Gus to kill that guy, do you?"

"That's how it looks. Maybe somebody hired Royster to do it, but he trained the bear."

"Maybe Gus just went crazy, got loose, and killed somebody."

"I wouldn't be surprised if that's the story Whip will try to give to the cops, but it won't make it true. If it makes you feel any better, I was about to turn Whip over to the cops anyway. You've just confirmed what I already suspected. Do yourself a favor, Archie, call the cops. You might get into hot water, but I don't think it'll be that bad. Stop withholding information. Take my advice. Please."

"I don't know, mister. I might just lam out of here."

"The cops will track you down. Listen, Whip's in trouble. Trust me, he'll sell you down river if he gets the chance. He'll tell the cops that you gave him a dangerous bear and didn't warn him properly. He'll put as much of the blame on you as he can."

"He's a pal."

"If it's proved he trained Gus to kill Cuthbert Hatfield, he could be charged with murder. He'll try to hang the killing on you. Go to the cops."

"Maybe. I got to think about it."

"I'm calling the cops right now. I'm telling them everything I've learned about this case, and I'm telling them everything you just told me. You're sunk. Your best plan is to come clean."

"I wish I was dead."

"No you don't. Things will be OK. You'll get through this. Thanks for calling me. Is there any way I can get ahold of you if I need to?"

"No. Like I said, I got no phone. I'm living in my car. Stinks of bear."

"You're living in your car in this weather?

You'll freeze."

"I'm doing OK. I run the heater some at nights. I got a warm coat."

"If you get too cold-call me. Maybe I can give you a place to stay for a couple of days."

"That's swell of you to offer. Do you mean it?"

"Of course. You're an OK guy, Archie. You just got in over your head."

"Wish I hadn't. Listen, I've been getting pretty cold the last few days. Would you really be willing to put me up for a while?"

"I said I would. I'll need to talk to my wife, but I'm sure she'll be OK with it. Come on over. I'll give you directions."

"Naw. I can't drive. The cops no doubt have the description of my car, and my license number. I'm sure my boss from the circus reported what I did."

"I haven't heard or read anything about it, but you're probably right. I'll pick you up. Where are you keeping your car?"

"Out in the warehouse district. There's a vacant lot with some old wrecked cars parked in it. I figured mine wouldn't be noticed."

"Give me an address."

"I don't know any of the addresses. The lot where I'm parked is near a place called Paxton Metal Products. You know where that is?"

"Not offhand. I'll look it up in the phone book. But you're at a phone booth right now, aren't you?"

"Yes. In a drugstore on Quarry Road. Harmon's

Pharmacy."

"I've got an idea where that is. Should I pick you up there?"

"My clothes and stuff are in my station wagon."

"OK. I'll pick you up at Harmon's and drive you over to your car so you can pick up your stuff. I can be at the drugstore in less than half-an-hour. Just stay put."

"You ain't going to call the cops on me, are you?"

"No. I promise. Hang tight. I'll pick you up."

"You're a great guy, Mr. Hatchett."

"Don't count on it. It could be I can use your help."

"I don't want Gus dead."

"We'll talk about it. Now, listen, don't get rabbit feet. I'm on the level here. I'm not going to turn you over to the cops. I'll see you in a little while. I'll be driving a blue Dodge pickup."

"I'll keep an eye out for it. Gee, thanks. Say, I don't have much money left. You might have to feed me."

"Swell. I hope you like sandwiches."

"I'll eat anything."

Archie hung up.

I went downstairs to the sandwich shop to talk to Tracy.

"We're going to have a non-paying boarder," I told her. I related the whole phone conversation to her.

"Maybe we can adopt him," she said. "Archie

can be our first kid. He can teach the kittens tricks."

"He's not an animal trainer. He's an electrician."

"Maybe he can fix our toaster."

I climbed into Bethany's truck, fired it up, and headed for the warehouse district. The snow had let up, but the roads were slippery. I wished I'd had some sandbags to put in the back of the pickup. Maybe Ben had some extras.

Harmon's Pharmacy was near the corner of Quarry and Excelsior. It was a dump needing paint. Archie must have been looking out the window for me because he came right out and opened the passenger door of the truck.

"Mr. Hatchett?"

"Call me Axe."

He climbed in. The truck's springs groaned. I don't know why I'd thought Archie would be a little guy. Something about his voice, I guess. He was about the size of Gus the Reaper, and smelled like him, too. I wasn't looking forward to feeding him.

"It sure is swell of you to take me in like this," Archie said.

"Forget it. Where's your car?"

He guided me through some side streets and to a large vacant lot featuring lots of snow and a dozen or so derelict cars. His station wagon turned out to be an old Cadillac hearse. I'd been wondering how he and the bear could have fit into a normal car. It must have been a beautiful boat at one time — it was a late thirties model — but the paint was wearing thin, and a couple of the fenders were crumpled.

"Doesn't it give you the willies driving a rig like that?" I asked him.

"No. She's a sweet ride."

He fetched a duffle bag from the death wagon and threw it into the back of the truck. On top of being big, Archie had flaming red hair and a matching beard. This guy couldn't manage to hide from the cops for long. I was surprised he hadn't been picked up already.

"How long have you been on the lam?" I asked.

"Almost three months, I guess. I ran out of cash about two months ago, but I picked up a part-time job loading bricks at one of the warehouses. They paid me under the table, and not much at that. But I've been able to eat."

"When we get back to my place, I'll fill you full of sandwiches."

"I'm kind of a big eater."

"I guessed as much. When did you turn the bear over to your pal, Royster?"

"More than two months ago. It was hard for me and Gus to be roommates in the old comfort wagon. Not to mention feeding him. I used to go through the trash cans behind a butcher shop, but Gus has an appetite even bigger than mine. And after a while the hearse started stinking of rotten meat and mangy bear. I had to take him out for walks at night. I didn't dare walk him in the daylight."

"Sounds like you've had a tough time. Things will get better. When's the last time you did your laundry?" He was dressed in overalls and a parka with a broken zipper. He smelled no worse than a dog food factory. "Mind you, I'm not complaining, but I figure your duds could use a good washing."

"I'll say. Sorry about the smell. They almost threw me out of the drugstore, but I think they were afraid of me. I'm a gentle guy, though, believe me."

"It was good of you to try to save Gus, but it didn't work out too well, did it?"

"Boy, you can say that again. Poor Gus. I didn't think Whip would train him up to kill a guy. He's a good bear, Gus is."

"Sure. He's just been running with the wrong crowd lately. Did the circus folks you work with consider giving Gus to a zoo? Quartz Quarry has one."

"They didn't think about it. They were trying to sell him to other circuses. A zoo's a great idea, though. Do you think it can still happen?"

"I hate to break your heart, Archie, but I think your pet bear is doomed. Still, we'll see what we can do. I know a newspaper guy, a reporter. I'll give him a call, see if he can put together a sweet story about Gus. Barney Lever's a good writer. He might be able to wring a few tears from the Quartz

Quarry citizens. But don't get your hopes up."

"I wish I could just go out in the woods and find Gus. I think he'd come to me. I could load him up in the station wagon and hit the road again."

"There's two things wrong with that plan. First, there's no way you could get that hearse up the roads around Flinders Cone. Second, you don't want to be on the lam for the rest of your life."

"I sure screwed things up, didn't I? But my mom always told me to look on the bright side, find the silver lining, watch for the rainbows."

"Where's your mom now?"

He gave a giant-sized sigh. "She passed on. She was walking down the street one day, and a piano fell on her. They were lowering it off of a three-story balcony and the rope broke."

"I'm sorry. So much for looking for rainbows."

15

When we got home, I took Archie into the sandwich shop. A few of the customers got a whiff of my new friend and lost their appetites.

"Come into our kitchen, Mr. Archie," Ben invited, when I'd made my introductions.

I gave Ben a ten-dollar bill. "Keep feeding him until he's full," I told Ben. "If you need more money let me know."

Ben pushed the bill back into my hand. "Mr. Archie is our guest. We'll feed him for you for free. Such a poor boy." I'd told Tracy, Ben, and Allie a little bit about the big fellow's circumstances.

When Archie was safely in the kitchen, Tracy whispered to me, "You didn't say you were bringing home a troll."

"How was I to know? He seems like a nice kid."

He wasn't really a kid. He might have been more than twenty-five, but there was something about the way he behaved that made him seem a lot younger.

171

"I hope he'll fit our guest bed," said Tracy, "and we'll need to scrub him down first." She had legitimate concerns on both counts. All we had for Archie to sleep on was Tracy's old single bed. It was a Princess bed. I hoped the big guy didn't mind. And our shower was designed for normal-sized folks, not Paul Bunyan's big brother.

I wolfed down a couple of sandwiches and headed to my office to use the phone. I called the offices of the Quartz Quarry Gladiator and asked for Barney Lever. He answered with his usual politeness.

"Barney!" he shouted when he got on the phone. "Make it snappy. I'm writing the best story of my life. My typewriter's almost turning into molten iron."

"I'll send over the fire department. This is Axe Hatchett."

"And what favor might you be asking for this time around?"

"I'm doing you a favor. I've got a great story for you. Not like whatever slop you're working on at the moment. I've got a giant for you to interview. And he's got a pet bear, named Gus, that's running around killing people. You interested?"

"Hell, yes! Sounds better than the pap I'm scribbling. Give me the details."

"You'll have to get them yourself. Come on over to my place and I'll arrange an interview."

"Bring him down to the Gladiator. You think my time's worth nothing?"

"I won't comment on that. Listen, let me warn you, this guy's a fugitive. The cops would love to nab him for stealing a killer bruin. Of course, I don't want to step on your delicate journalistic sensibilities. Forget everything I just told you. Lovely day, isn't it?"

"You're asking me to forget the story? Two fugitives from justice — one of them a bear? I'll be right over. Give me the address."

"Leave your camera at the office."

"What camera? I'll be over in a couple of hours. I've got a deadline to meet."

He hung up.

I decided to haul Archie's duffle bag full of dirty clothes down to the local Laundromat, which is only a couple of blocks from our place. I dropped into the sandwich shop and told Tracy what was going on.

"He'll still be eating when you get back," she said.

While I was loading Archie's huge and smelly clothing into the fortunately large washing machines, I thought about what I was getting myself into. Not only was I now hampered with a two-legged Clydesdale for a roommate, I was also willfully harboring a fugitive. What was in it for me? Would this guy be able to help me solve the murder of Cuthbert Hatfield, and maybe aid in rounding up the bear?

I hoped so, but my expectations weren't too sunny. I feared there might not be a silver lining.

Maybe something more like a falling piano.

I got Archie's clothes washed and dried, and returned to the apartment where I had the bear-napper safely ensconced. Barney hadn't shown up yet. Archie was holed-up in our guest room and gleefully grabbed some of his clean clothes and took them into the bathroom for a long-overdue shower.

He came out smelling as sweet as a rosebud, but he still had his big red beard. He'd been keeping his hair clipped — maybe with a mule shears — and wore some fetching bangs. He looked like an overgrown Dutch boy.

"Did you grow that while you've been on the run?" I asked him.

"No. I've had this beard for years."

"Then you need to get rid of it. Say, you haven't gone two or three months without a shower, have you?"

"I washed up in a creek sometimes, when it was warm enough."

I fetched a scissors and introduced Archie to my safety razor.

"Try not to use up my whole packet of blades," I said, and sent him back into the bathroom.

Barney showed up while Archie was still removing the fur from his face. My reporter friend was around forty, bald except for a closely-clipped fringe of ginger hair. Barney was a born cynic, but he could write up a story as sweet and sappy as you could possibly want. While Archie was still in the bathroom, I filled Barney in on the tale of the stolen bear.

"This guy just grabbed the bear and ran?" asked Barney. "Stuffed it in his hearse and found a hide-away?"

"That's right."

"OK. I can't figure the cops have been looking very hard for him. You say he's a red-headed gi-ant? With a four-hundred-pound bear and a fancy Cadillac hearse? Shouldn't be too difficult to run a guy like that to ground. The cops, they ain't earn-ing their fat paychecks.

"Just so we'll be clear about this, I handled this whole interview over the phone. Get it? Mr. Pall called me and gave me the story. I don't know where he can be found."

"Of course. Neither one of us has ever seen this Archie Pall guy."

"Perzactly. You got any rye?"

I didn't. Barney had to settle for coffee.

When Archie emerged from the bathroom, Bar-ney's jaw dropped open.

"Hello, Mr. Paul Bunyan," he greeted the big guy.

Except for his size, Archie was hardly recog-nizable. His doughy baby face was shorn of its fur. He'd cut himself in two or three places and had stopped the bleeding with little patches of toilet paper. The lower half of his face was fish-belly white, but in a few days he'd look like a guy who had never worn a beard. And he'd trimmed his hair up more.

Barney shook hands with Archie, wincing a bit, then pulled a small notebook and a pencil from one pocket of his garish plaid sports coat. "So, big guy, give me the news."

Archie told Barney the same tale he'd delivered to me, and Barney busily scribbled in his notebook, a gleeful smile lighting his face. When the interview was over, he read back some of his notes to us.

"How's this?" he asked us. "'Gus, the bear, a gentle giant who delights in wagging his stubby tail at awe-struck children, is in trouble.

"A sweet-natured teddy bear who has never in the past laid tooth or nail on any of his handlers, Gus recently snuffed the scent of one of his wild brothers.

"Confused, Gus became depressed and failed to perform up to his callous trainer's unreasonable standards. Frustrated by repeated beatings, Gus nipped the keeper's arm, carefully covering his fearsome fangs with his gums.

"Overreacting, the circus proprietors who had enslaved this cuddly bruin, determined to cold-bloodedly exterminate poor Gus. But an electrician, who works for the circus, and who wouldn't give me his name over the phone, came to Gus's rescue.

"After futilely begging his money-grubbing employers to give Gus to our fine local zoo — check out the swell elephants next time you visit

Quartz Quarry's splendid menagerie! — the nameless thunder-bolt-handler was forced to steal Gus in order to save the bear's life.

"Yes, steal!

"This model employee was pushed into a criminal act in order to spare the life of a pet bear he'd grown to love as a brother.

"But this wasn't the end of Gus's travails. The electrician found a new home for the bear, passing him on to a foul villain who he thought was a trusted friend.

"This 'friend' owns a pricey estate in the country. The bear's electrician pal hoped that Gus would spend his remaining days happily romping through flower-dotted meadows. But this was not to be.

"Gus's new owner treated the bruin savagely, forcing him to become a killer. The victim? Cuthbert Hatfield. You've read the details in our fine newspaper.

"But is Gus to blame? No! He was forced to commit the act that ended Hatfield's life.

"This bear deserves a second chance in my opinion. Let's round him up and provide him with a new home at the zoo.

"No doubt, Gus is feeling guilt-stricken, but in time he might become his own carefree, happy, self again. And we'll all benefit from that.'"

"That's a great story," said Archie. "And part of it's true."

"Sure," said Barney. "And if this story doesn't

dump a libel suit on the Gladiator, everything will be the hunkiest of doriest."

"Thanks, Barney," I said. "I owe you one."

The article, with some further embellishments, appeared in the Gladiator the next morning.

Now what? I could let the cops take care of everything. Or I could try to find the guy who'd tried to kill me and could have hurt my Tracy. Or I could interrogate Whip until he cracked and told me everything. I could also try to track down Gus the Reaper and turn him over to the zoo. Or ask the Forest Service to do it.

Or I could just sit back and eat sandwiches and do nothing — twiddle my thumbs. Clean the cat box.

Instead, I decided to keep investigating. Keep dodging bullets. I called Bethany.

"I'm snow-bound," she complained. "Talk to me."

I told her about Archie Pall and what he'd told me, though I didn't say he was living with us.

"Do you think Whip really trained that bear to kill Cuthbert?"

"Yes. But I'm guessing somebody paid him to do it. That's the person I need to find."

"You'll get shot at again. Maybe the guy's aim will be better next time. Why don't you give it up?"

"You don't want me to find out who's responsible for your brother's death?"

"I want to know, yes. But it sounds like it's in

the hands of the police now. Why not let them handle it?"

"They've got other things to do, and I've got nothing else. Just this case."

"Are you asking me if I'll keep you on the payroll?"

"Yes, I guess that's what I'm asking."

"Sure. I'm still willing to finance your investigation. But I don't want your death on my conscience. Shouldn't you just hole up for a while?"

"I'll have to in this weather. But I can make some phone calls. I don't like just sitting around."

"Do what you think is best. But please be careful."

"I'll guard my life as if it were my own."

She laughed. It was like angel fish wriggling through tropical waters. That was worth the phone call. I thought of something else to ask her.

"Who do you know who has money, and who also knows Ambrose and knew Cuthbert?"

"I've already told you Whip Royster might have some money. And Harvey Rundell."

"Seriously? What'd Harvey do with his dough — bury it in the backyard?"

"Knowing Harvey, that's a possibility. A few years ago, Harvey's wife was killed in a car accident. The kid driving the other car was drunk, and he didn't have a license, but mom and dad had a lot of money. I think they talked Harvey into settling out of court. Of course, I have no idea how much money Harvey got out of the deal."

"Maybe enough to hire someone who owns a killer bear. I'll have to give him a call. I've already talked to him, but I didn't know he had money then."

"I can't think of anyone else familiar with my brothers who's well-heeled."

"At least you came up with a couple of names. Thanks. I'll keep in touch."

"Do that. I want to know everything you find out."

We ended the call.

I thought of calling Ambrose. He might just hang up on me, but so what? I dialed his number.

16

"This is Hatfield."

"Axe Hatchett."

"What the hell do you want?"

"I want to warn you. I've found some things out about that bear. Its name is Gus. It was stolen from a circus. They were about to put it down because it was getting dangerous. Stay away from it. Don't try tracking it anymore."

"Don't tell me what to do. You're as bad as my sister."

"Oh? Has she been warning you?"

"She calls me five times a day. In fact, I thought it was her calling me now. But you're even worse."

"You can't blame her. Her brother just got killed by Gus the Reaper. By the way, Bethany told me the bear was trying to kill you. It jumped on your back."

"That's right. Cuthbert saved me, the fool."

"You'd have done the same for him."

"Maybe. But I wouldn't have gotten killed doing it."

"It must make you feel pretty bad."

"I'll feel better when I've killed that bear. Gus. Who'd name a bear Gus?"

"Who cares? Say, by the way, would you happen to know who dropped by my place and took a couple of shots at me?"

"Sounds like a good idea, but I didn't do it, if that's what you're thinking."

"Where were you about eight-thirty last night?"

"Sitting in front of my fire."

"Can you prove it?"

"I don't need to prove nothing to nobody. You hear?"

"Don't hang up. I'm not through with you. The cops recovered the two slugs that were fired at me. One of them smashed on the brick wall. But the other one struck my wooden door," I lied. "It's in pretty good shape. They can probably tell what gun fired it."

"If they find the gun."

"You own a forty-five handgun?"

"Of course I do. Cuthbert owned one too."

"The cops might visit you."

"They can go to hell. I didn't shoot at you. If I had, I'd have killed you."

"You've missed the bear twice."

"I hit him the second time. I'm sure of it."

"Find any blood?"

"No, and I can't figure it out."

"Maybe Gus is wearing a bullet-proof vest."

"Don't be an idiot. I'm going to hang up now. Between you and Bethany, I'm not getting no peace."

"We're both trying to protect you."

"No. Bethany wants me to sell part of my land. Cuthbert gets killed, and she doesn't even wait a day to start pushing! Wants me to go along with some land sale she's working on."

"I thought she inherited her own land. Why should she need your permission to sell?"

"She can do whatever the hell she wants with her land, but the guy who wants to buy it wants to buy the land that borders it. I own that land. The guy doesn't want to go through with the deal unless he can buy both parcels of property."

"Why does Bethany need to sell anything? She's well-fixed, isn't she?"

"The princess? Sure. But she'll never have enough money. She like houses, cars, jewelry, clothes. She spends like a fiend."

"I see. Was she trying to push through this land deal while Cuthbert was alive?'

"Yeah, but now she's really putting on the heat. My answer's no, and it's going to stay no."

"Who's the guy who wants to buy the land?"

"What business is it of yours?"

"It's my business because I'm still trying to find out who trained the bear that killed your brother. I'm still on the case, even without your money. Come on, Ambrose, quit being pig-headed. Don't you want to know who's responsible for Cuthbert's death?"

"Why would Grover Templer want to kill my brother over some land deal?"

"Templer of Templer and Dial Real Estate? Is that the guy Bethany is working with? He's got a lousy reputation, and — from what I hear — he doesn't like taking no for an answer. He's full of money. He might sic a bear on you and Cuthbert to scare you into the land sale, if he thought you could guess he was behind it. And I hear he's got the mayor in his watch pocket. And the cops would leave him alone unless they had absolute proof of what he was up to. I'm going to call this Templar guy, maybe go out to see him."

"Oh, that'll put a scare in him. Dick Tracy to the rescue."

He slammed down the receiver. But he'd given me a couple of things to think about. The bear, for instance. Ambrose had shot at it twice, and both times he'd been convinced that he'd hit it. What if Gus really was wearing a bulletproof vest? Whip could have made one. He could have taken an old bear hide, dyed it if necessary, and stitched some steel plates onto the back of it.

Gus could wear it like a saddle. It could be made like a jacket. It would protect the bear's chest and sides. Why not? And maybe the hump on his back was just stuffing, to make him look like a grizzly bear. I'd heard of stranger things. Though, admittedly, not many.

The second thing I had to think about was Bethany and this Templar guy. So, she needed money, and was in a big hurry to sell part of her property. But she needed Ambrose to cooperate in selling some of his property as well. And he was pig-headed. But if he were dead, he'd be much more co-operative.

Actually, the property would come into his ex-wife's hands. If Kelly could prove that selling the land would benefit her sons, then the deal could go through.

How much did Bethany really love her brothers? She'd spoken about them in pretty negative terms. What if she'd found out about Gus when Whip had adopted him? Melinda had dated Whip, and Bethany was a woman who would just love poaching another woman's man. What if she had become Whip's lover and had learned about the bear? She could have hired him to train Gus to kill Ambrose. But maybe Gus's nose wasn't good enough to tell the difference between Cuthbert and Ambrose. Hell, I didn't know.

But then why would Bethany hire me? To keep close track of the case, that's why. And maybe she felt I was getting too close to the truth. So she'd hired someone, maybe Whip, to ambush me in front of my own apartment. She'd dropped me off only a few minutes before the shooting. Maybe he'd missed his chance when I'd stepped from the car, but decided to stick around a while longer to see if I'd show myself as a target one more time. It made sense, or as much sense as such things like that ever make. It's hard to get inside the head of a murderer.

I looked out my front office window. The snow had slowed to a light confetti, but the roads were likely still a mess. I grabbed my well-thumbed phone book and looked up a couple of numbers. I made my first call to Templar and Dial Real Estate. I had expected a sweet-voiced receptionist to answer, but it was a guy, and he sounded cranky.

"Templer and Dial."

"Could I speak with Grover Templer?"

"You'll have to try his house. He's snowed in. So is the damned receptionist. This is Dexter Dial. Can I help you?"

"No. I need to speak to Grover. I just tried his home phone and nobody answered. Maybe the phone lines are down."

"If it wasn't for the weather, I'd say he was out golfing. Can I take a message?"

"Well, I guess that would be all right. Let's see. How about this. Tell him: 'One down and one to go. Gus is loose and has a mind of his own.' Say, that kind of rhymes, doesn't it? Give him that message. Those exact words. Have him call me back at the number I'm going to give you. It's a sandwich shop, but never mind that. Tell him to ask for Tracy. Got it?"

"What's all this secret agent crap about? What's Grover up to?"

"He's your partner. Ask him."

I hung up.

I went over to the sandwich shop to warn Tracy about the call she was going to get. I kept looking for gunmen during the brief time I was outside.

"What's all this about?" Tracy asked.

"Just throwing out some bait. Write down whatever the guy says to you."

"You going to pay me?"

"With kisses. Here's one in advance."

I went back to my office. My next call was to Harvey Rundell. He answered on about the seventeenth ring.

"This is Harvey."

"Mr. Rundell? My name's Axe Hatchett. I'm a private investigator."

"Oh? What do you want?"

"I want to talk to you about a bear. He recently killed a man up in your area. A Cuthbert Hatfield."

"I heard about that. Terrible! I haven't seen the bear."

"No? He's running around your neighborhood, wreaking havoc. I have it on good authority the bear's name is Gus. He's a big, hump-backed, beast, kind of brown-and-blond. If you see him, give me a call. I'll give you my number. We're afraid he might kill the remaining brother."

"He sure killed the wrong brother. Smeller must be off. Ambrose is the bad one."

"That so? I understand the bear is in the guardianship of a certain Whip Royster. But we can't find the guy. Would you happen to know where he is?"

There was silence on the line for a spell. Then Harvey spoke.

"Whip's disappeared? What makes you think he had the bear? It's wild."

"It's no more wild than you, Mr. Rundell. It's a trained bear. It was stolen from a circus. Mr. Royster may have enhanced the bear's training. He may have taught it to kill the Hatfield brothers by tracking them down by sent."

"You think Whip did that?"

"Yes, but someone might have hired him to do it."

"Say, you sound familiar. Have I talked to you before?"

"No. By the way, Mr. Rundell, how's fishing?"

I hung up. I was just playing around.

Tracy came into my office, coatless.

"I got a message for you," she said. "A Mr. Templer called and asked for me. He said to tell the practical joker who'd left a message for him to find something better to do on snowy days. 'Try coloring books', he said."

"Thanks, porcupine. That gives me the last piece of the puzzle."

"Really? That's exciting!"

"I'm lying."

"Oh. How's the case going for real?"

"Slow as a sloth with a wooden leg."

"I got to get back to my customers."

"You have customers — with these roads?"

"Sure. Folks have to eat. Speaking of eaters, how's Archie doing?"

"OK, I guess. He seems restless. He's doing a lot of pacing. I'm surprised you can't hear it downstairs. I'm thinking of taking him out for a little ride later."

"On these roads? Don't forget his leash."

"It'll be all right. His extra weight will give Bethany's truck better traction."

"If Archie gets bored, tell him he can fix our toaster."

"He already fixed it. And he's teaching the kittens tricks."

"Great! Will they be able to jump through flaming hoops?"

"Let's hope not."

She kissed me and headed for the door.

"Watch out for gunmen," I said, and I meant it.

I thought about my conversation with Harvey Rundell. We'd been talking about Cuthbert getting killed, and Harvey'd said: "He sure killed the wrong brother. Smeller must be off." How did Harvey know that Ambrose was supposed to be the brother who died? He couldn't have known unless he'd hired Whip to sic the bear on Ambrose. I could feel the pieces of the puzzle all coming together.

However, I needed a confession, and I wasn't the person who could get it. But I knew who could. A femme fatale who could get any guy to squirm and spill his guts. I called Bethany.

"How are your feminine wiles holding up?" I asked her.

"I've still got what I was born with. Why?"

"I know who killed your brother. Harvey Rundell. And Whip provided the murder weapon."

"My God! Are you sure?"

"My gut says so, but my gut's mostly for digesting cheese burgers."

"Why would Harvey want Ambrose dead? I mean, more than others would?"

"He likes to fish. You never know what's going to set a guy off. Harvey's a strange one, and he's not above breaking the law. I want you to do me a favor. I want you to bat your lovely eyelashes and jiggle your cushiony bosom."

"For you?"

"Don't even think about it. I want you to wring a confession out of Harvey, or Whip, or both. Think you're up to it?"

"I don't mind a challenge. I can give it a shot. Might be kind of fun."

"Try getting in touch with those two boys and let me know what happens."

"If you're right about Harvey causing Cuthbert's death, I owe you a big fat paycheck."

"I'll be looking forward to cashing it."

I still wasn't certain about Harvey Rundell's being behind the murder, and I had a bear to catch. Archie was napping and I woke him up.

"How did Gus behave when he was with you?"

I asked him. "Peaceful?"

"Like a pet poodle. Why?"

"Do you think you could talk him into coming to you? Do his keepers use a dog whistle on him, or what?"

"Dog whistle? No. They use voice commands and hand signals." He perked up. "You saying you want to go rescue Gus?"

"Yes, but not if he's going to turn on us and kill us. He's tasted man blood now, and he might be a different bear from what he was. I'm taking my twelve-gauge, loaded with double-ought buckshot. I'm warning you, I'll shoot him if I have to."

"It won't come to that. I know Gus. I don't know how Whip managed to train him to kill that poor guy, but Gus has a good nature."

"I sure as hell hope you're right. Grab your coat, we're going."

We stopped in at the sandwich shop and bought a sack of sandwiches for the road, and two thermoses of coffee.

"We're going bear hunting." I told Tracy.

"You're going to kill poor Gus?"

"Don't forget his other name is Reaper. We're going to try to capture him, keep him from killing Ambrose or anyone else. But if Archie can't talk sense into that bear, and it charges us, I'm afraid I'll have to shoot him."

"Don't worry, Mrs. Hatchett," said Archie, "I know I can handle Gus. We'll bring him back to town and maybe the zoo will take him. I hope my old boss won't cause trouble. But why the hell wouldn't he be willing to give Gus to the zoo? It's better than killing him."

"Bring him back in one piece," Tracy told Archie. "Bring my husband back in one piece, too. Don't forget all the sandwiches we've given you."

I kissed Tracy goodbye, I hoped not for the last time, and Archie and I swept the snow off of Bethany's truck and headed off for the woods. On our way out of town we stopped at a hardware store and bought a coil of thick rope. Archie had also acquired some pastrami that was turning green from Ben and Allie. For bear bait.

17

The roads were hell. They were bad enough in town, but up in the mountains they were slippery, and snow-covered, and hard to navigate. The truck slid around all over and got stuck twice. However, Archie, with his beefy shoulders, was able to push the truck out of the places where we got bogged down. He was like a gorilla that's been working out in the gym.

We ploughed our way up to the Hatfield property, but we didn't go too near the house. I didn't want to see Ambrose, and I didn't want him seeing us. We made our way on foot to the place where Gus the Reaper had chased me and the Hatfield brothers up trees. I figured it was as good a spot as any to start our search.

Archie and I tramped around in the woods for a good two hours, looking for bear tracks and hollering Gus's name at the top of our lungs. No luck. We didn't see any tracks. If Gus was around, he chose to ignore our calling him. Archie waved the

bad pastrami around in the air, but it only attract-
ed an aged raccoon.

"I give up," I told Archie. "We'll come back another day. Let's get back to the truck. I'm freez-
ing."

"Let's just look a little longer," Archie begged.
"Gus might be feeling shy."

"We haven't seen any tracks. I don't think he's
anywhere near here. Let's go eat our sandwiches."

We slogged back to Bethany's pickup, ate our
sandwiches, and enjoyed the heater. I was just getting ready to take us back to town when I got an
idea. I think it'd been rattling around in my head
for some time. It was a silly idea, but sometimes
those are the best kind. I turned to Archie.

"We're going to pay a little visit to Ambrose
Hatfield," I told him.

I'd parked the truck within half-a-mile of the
Hatfield place, so I now drove up the rest of the
way. Archie was moving nervously on the seat.

"What's wrong?" I asked.

"I'm not sure I want to meet this guy. You
didn't make him sound very friendly."

"It'll be OK. Stop worrying. I've got a shotgun
don't I?"

Ambrose's Jimmy was in the yard and I parked
next to it, but I didn't take the shotgun to the
house. I did have Ben's six-shooter in my coat
pocket, though. We went up on the porch and I
knocked. A light fall of snow was swirling around
in the air. The door suddenly jerked open.

"What're you doing here, Hatchett? Get off my property."

The two dogs appeared behind the disgruntled Ambrose and spilled out the door. They wrapped themselves around me and Archie's legs, wiggling their tails.

"Damned fine guard dogs I've got," said Ambrose. He jerked his chin at my companion. "You bring that big fellow out here to beat me up? He don't have a chance."

"I just want to look at your game room," I said. "It's about Cuthbert's murder. I think I know who did it."

Ambrose snorted. "Fat lot of good that does me."

"Come on, Hatfield, let us in. I'm not taking no for an answer."

"Ain't you?"

He stepped out the door, fast. I got a doubled-up fist in my belly. I could feel each one of my sandwiches getting squashed against my spine. I backed up a step and tried to recover my breath. God, that punch hurt.

By the time I recovered, Ambrose was starting on Archie. But that was a mistake. Ambrose rained punches on the giant's midsection and Archie ignored them. He stuck out a big hand and grabbed Ambrose by the collar. Then he lifted him off his feet and shook him.

That was more than Doc and Spotty were willing to take. They fastened their teeth onto Archie's lower leg. Archie dropped Ambrose and carefully unclamped the dogs' jaws from his thick coveralls.

"Good boys," he said. "I was just funning with your master."

Ambrose came at me again. He took a round-house swing and I ducked under it and stepped in close to him. I gave him a right uppercut to the chin with everything I could muster behind it. Ambrose fell on his back and shook his head a few times.

"Damn it, Ambrose, grow up," I said. "I'm here for something important." I walked around his prostrate form and went into the house. Over my shoulder I said to Archie: "Watch him for me."

Nothing in the big house had changed. The checkerboard was still on the table. I wondered if Ambrose had been playing checkers by himself. The place smelled like whiskey and burned stew.

I headed to the game room. Behind me I could hear Ambrose giving Archie a piece of his mind, but I didn't hear the sound of fists. I went over to the bearskin rug on the floor and picked it up. It was heavier than I'd expected. I draped it over a table. I wished I'd brought a magnifying glass, but my naked eyes would have to do.

I carefully examined the bear's teeth. I hadn't been wrong: there were tiny specks of dried blood on some of the fangs and a reddish-brown spot on the varnished tongue. I went into the living room. To my surprise Ambrose and Archie were seated at the table and Ambrose was pouring whiskey into two glasses.

"Mr. Hatfield wants to know what the hell you're up to," Archie told me, mildly.

"Glad you boys are getting along," I said. "You got a third glass for that whiskey?"

"Thought you didn't drink," said Ambrose.

"This is a special occasion. Pour me a couple of fingers."

He did. When he handed me the glass, he almost smiled. "That was a good punch. I always heard you detectives could fight."

"You've got a pretty good gut punch yourself."

The three of us sat at the table and sipped our whiskey like gentlemen. Ambrose was through being angry. He rolled and lit a cigarette. I fired up a cigar. Archie produced a pouch of Beechnut chewing tobacco and stuffed a wad in his cheek.

"Don't spit on my floor, young fellow."

"No, sir. I'll spit in the fire."

Ambrose turned to me. "Now tell me why you broke into my place."

"I didn't break in. I just stepped over your body and walked through the open door."

"Yeah. What for?"

"I wanted to take a good look at that big bear-skin rug in your game room. I'd remembered those two drops of dried blood on the floor you'd once pointed out to me. You and your brother weren't getting along too well towards the last, were you?"

"I don't figure it's none of your business. But,

you're right. Cuthbert was getting soft. He kept whining at me about the way I treat folks. And he was ragging at me to sell a piece of land of mine."

"The land that border's Bethany's? Was this part of that land sale she was hoping to complete?"

"That's right. Wouldn't leave me alone about it. Called me stubborn."

"Imagine that."

"Didn't like the way I acted. I don't know what got in to him these last few months. I wonder if he'd met a woman. He was as spineless as a bowl of mush. We fought some. Now, what does this have to do with a bearskin?"

"Your brother hired Whip Royster to train a bear — "

"Gus," said Archie.

"To train a bear — named Gus — to kill you. I figured he hated you towards the end."

"You don't know what you're saying. Cuthbert was my brother. We shared the same blood. We had a few fistfights, he even pulled a knife on me once, but he wouldn't have wanted me dead."

"I think you're wrong. When I examined the bearskin rug I found traces of blood on the teeth. How'd they get there?"

"From Cuthbert's wounded leg."

"Not likely. How would it end up on the bear's teeth? Here's what happened. Cuthbert hired Whip to train Gus the Reaper to maul you. Your brother was afraid of being traced to the crime, so he came up with a way to make it look like the bear was actually out to kill him.

"One day, when you had gone to town, he took that bearskin and worried his own leg with its teeth. Must have been painful, and bloody, but that's what he did. Then he cleaned up as best as he could and waited for you to return.

"He gave you that story about being attacked by the Reaper — Gus — and having his leg chewed on. But he said he was so shook up that when he went back to retrieve his lost cap he couldn't find the spot where the bear attacked him. Couldn't find the tree he'd climbed. Couldn't find the bear's tracks. There weren't any tracks."

"You're crazier than an owl."

"Maybe, but that doesn't change what happened. Do you ever use a dog whistle on your dogs?"

"Sometimes, but they don't pay no attention."

"The day Cuthbert was killed, he had a dog whistle in his pocket. It fell out when his body was being carried to the paddy wagon. I think he was using that whistle to try to control the bear. Whip Royster could handle Gus, but your brother couldn't.

"The day you were attacked, Gus was doing exactly what Whip had trained him to do. But when the bear jumped on your back, Cuthbert lost his nerve. He couldn't stand by and watch his brother get mauled to death. He tried to save you, and the confused bear went for him."

"I don't believe a word of it," said Ambrose.

"Suit yourself, but the cops might listen to me. And I wouldn't be surprised if they wring a confession out of Whip."

I finished my whiskey and stood up. "Time to go, Archie." I took a last look at Ambrose. "I'm sorry your brother hated you enough to want you dead, but in the end he saved your life. I've got a few words of advice for you: leave that bear alone. Quit hunting him."

"I'll do what I damned well please. I'm a Hatfield."

"Thanks for the hooch," I said.

"Thank you for the nice whiskey, Mr. Hatfield," said Archie.

We returned to the truck and slithered our way back to town.

Back in my office, I called Bethany.

"How'd you make out with Rundell and Royster?" I asked her, when she answered.

She laughed, like cool water tinkling into a lotus pool. "What an unfortunate choice of words, Axe. I didn't make out with either of the boys. I only talked to them on the phone. Neither of them were very informative."

"I think I've got Royster over a barrel. And we can forget about Harvey. I think I know who's responsible for your brother's death."

"Who? Tell me."

"Cuthbert himself."

"You mean because he threw himself on the bear when he was trying to save Ambrose?"

"No. I think Cuthbert hired Whip Royster to train the bear to kill Ambrose."

She was silent for a time, then: "How could that be? My brothers didn't always get along, but they were devoted to each other."

"That changed towards the end. Do you know of any women Cuthbert might have been romantically involved with recently?"

"I don't. If Cuthbert had a girlfriend, he was keeping her a secret."

I told her about the bearskin and the blood.

"You might be right, or you might be chasing a wild goose."

"I know. Whip knows who hired him, of course. We need to go after Whip."

"Have you talked to the police?"

"Not yet. I wanted to talk to you first. I wanted to know what you thought of my idea."

"I'll have to think about it. I must admit it comes as a shock."

"I know, and I'm sorry. But I think I'm right."

We ended the conversation, and I called the cops. I don't like talking to the brave boys in blue — they're too brittle, and they think they know everything — so I called the girl in blue. I called Blythe Bliss.

"Bliss Speaking."

"This is Axe."

"What do you want from me now?"

"I only want to give you the name of a murderer."

"I know the names of several."

"You don't know this guy's name. It's Whip Royster. He lives up by Flinders Cone. He used to be an animal trainer. I believe Cuthbert Hatfield hired Whip to train the bear that ended up killing Cuthbert himself."

"You've got evidence?"

"Yes. I know the guy who gave up the bear to Whip Royster. I'm protecting him. You and your brave lads need to go after Whip and baby a confession out of him."

"If I start that ball rolling, I'll look like a fool if you're wrong."

"I'd bet a nickel's worth of twenty-dollar bills that I'm right."

"I'll see what I can do. I just hope you don't make a laughing stock out of me."

"You're safe. Let me know what your stalwart comrades find out, will you?"

"Sure. Tell your wife and the kittens that Blythe said howdy."

"I will. You'll thank me for this. I hope. We'll have you over for chow sometime."

My belly told me it was time to eat. I stepped over to the sandwich shop.

"How's the case going?" Tracy asked me. She had a dab of mayonnaise on her cheek and I kissed it off.

"I think I might have solved it."

I told her what I knew, and what my speculations were.

"So Cuthbert brought about his own death. Didn't Shakespeare mention something like that in one of his plays? It's been a long time since I was in high school."

"Hamlet. It looks like Cuthbert was 'hoist on his own petard.'"

"Whatever that means. You did a lot of reading when you were in jail, didn't you?"

"Yeah. There wasn't much else to do. Do you think you can round up enough leftover sandwiches for me and you and the big boy upstairs?"

"I think we'll have a bunch. How's Archie doing?"

"He's a little blue right now because we didn't find Gus."

"Maybe Gus decided to hibernate."

"That's a thought worth thinking! I'm going upstairs."

18

The next couple of days brought nothing. Then Blythe called me.

"A little birdy told me a few things this morning," she said.

"What kind of bird?"

"A buzzard with sergeant's stripes. Your Whip Royster is behind bars, bless his heart. We were able to coax a confession out of him."

"I won't ask how."

"There's not a mark on him."

"Rubber hoses are convenient that way."

"We have gentler ways to get people to talk. We lied and told him we already knew that Cuthbert Hatfield had hired him to train the bear. He caved in after a while. So I guess you were right."

"Thanks. I know that's hard for you to say. So the case is wrapped up?"

"With a bow and everything. So what are you going to do now?"

"Learn how to embroider."

"Could you do a pillow case for me?"

"Sure. With the police department's insignia on it."

"I'll hold my breath."

I collected a big fat paycheck from Bethany, and a big fat kiss. I didn't tell Tracy about the latter, but she was happy about the former.

Archie grew more and more restless and finally turned himself in. He got sixty days in the calaboose for stealing the bear. Tracy and I visited him when we could and brought him sandwiches. He really liked the peanut butter and turkey breast creation Tracy had invented.

For months Gus eluded all efforts to find him. Hibernation seemed the likeliest explanation.

In June, when Archie was sprung from his cage he found a job working for a small appliance shop. He stayed with us for a little while and then moved into his own tiny apartment. He borrowed Bethany's truck a few times — she'd met him through me and Tracy and appeared to adore him —and went off to the hills to search for Gus. Sometimes, if I wasn't working, I'd go with him.

On a bright day in late May Archie and I drove up to Flinders Cone again. I'd given up on finding Gus, but Archie had his mom's sunny outlook on life.

"I'm sure we'll find him," he told me. "Last time I was up here I spotted a cave opening. You could just barely see it from this old dirt road. But when I hiked up to look for it I couldn't find it. I figure today you can stand down by the road and kind of guide me while I climb up to look. We can holler back and forth."

"Sure, just like a couple of hillbillies. We should have brought a jug of corn squeezin's to share."

"Don't sound so down about it, Mr. Hatchett." I'd asked him over and over again to call me Axe, but he felt beholden to me and Tracy, and insisted on addressing us respectfully. "I think we'll find Gus today, I really do."

I grunted something, and thought about pianos falling off balconies.

We found the dirt track Archie said he'd spotted the cave from, and drove down it a good half mile.

"There it is!" Archie pointed at something and made me stop the truck. We got out and craned our necks, and Archie kept pointing until I finally saw a ragged hole in the face of a rock cliff about fifty yards up the side of a steep hill. The big guy grabbed a small coil of rope from the truck bed.

"I'm going up," he said. "You wait down here and yell directions at me."

"You'll break your neck climbing up there."

"No I won't. I'm light on my feet. My sister was a ballerina in high school."

"I hope they had a nice sturdy stage for her to dance on."

"She ain't big like me. Aggie's just a little bit of a thing."

I really didn't want to think about Archie's family.

"Go ahead and climb, then, but watch yourself. Tracy would kill me if I let anything happen to you."

"Mrs. Hatchett's the nicest lady I've ever known, next to Mom."

"I kind of like her myself. Get going. The wind is coming up."

It was June already and the sun was shining, but there were still big patches of old snow in the hills. The wind that was blowing across them was chilly as a head waiter in a swank eatery.

"Wish me luck," said Archie, and started his climb.

He climbed like a mountain goat — in ballet slippers — but got sidetracked a couple of times and never would have found the cave opening if I hadn't been yelling at him where to go. He was only a few yards from the cave when I heard a noise behind me. A chuffing, snuffling, sound. I felt about a ton of ice forming on my backbone.

I turned around very slowly. Gus was standing about five yards away, smiling. At least I hoped it was a smile. He looked like he could use a hairbrush, and part of his hide seemed to be slipping off his back. The damned bulletproof vest Whip Royster had admitted to having made for the bear. There were leaves stuck in Gus's fur, and he was gaunt. He was obviously hungry.

I turned my head a little, still keeping the bear in sight, and yelled over my shoulder at Archie.

"Hey! Archie! Come on down! I've got company!" I got the feeling my voice carried pretty well.

Archie stared down at me, then cupped his hands around his gawping mouth and shouted. "Don't move, Mr. Hatchett! I'm on my way!"

He climbed, and slithered, and practically somersaulted down the steep hillside. Before I knew it, he was standing next to me, breathing hard and sweating. Gus walked right past me and nuzzled Archie's outstretched hand. If he'd been a dog, and had a decent amount of tail, he would have wagged a hello.

"Keep him busy, will you?" I asked Archie. "I'm going to sneak over and grab my shotgun from the truck."

"Don't, Mr. Hatchett. He's friendly. See? Come pet him. Come pat Gus."

I would rather have petted a sub-machine gun with a cobra wrapped around it, but I couldn't let Archie know I was shaking in my loafers. The big guy looked up to me, in a manner of speaking. I took a few cowardly steps backwards and then steeled myself and headed over to Gus.

"Nice Gus," I said, soothingly. "Good boy." I patted him on his padded hump and he shook himself a little. He didn't growl, though, and I had hopes I'd keep all my fingers.

"What's he got strapped on him?" Archie asked.

"His bulletproof vest, remember? I told you about it."

"I forgot. We got to get it off of him. He must be itching like crazy."

"If I unfold my jackknife, he won't get the wrong idea, will he?"

"Just move slow. Poor Gus is all confused. He doesn't know who his friends are. But you're with me. You're fine."

I took out my knife and got closer to Gus than I wanted to. At the last second I lost my nerve and handed the knife to Archie. "Here, you cut the thing off of him."

"How's it fastened on I wonder?." He investigated and found a couple of straps all tangled in Gus's fur. He cut through them with my knife and pulled off the whole saddle-like pad. As soon as the vest hit the ground Gus shook himself like a rain-soaked poodle, and then laid down in the road on his back and squirmed around. He let out some very loud grunts that I hoped were friendly.

Poor Gus," said Archie. "That thing must have been killing him. We found him, Mr. Hatchett! We found good old Gus."

"And what exactly are we going to do with good old Gus? Take him to the YMCA?"

"Let's take him to your place. It's bigger than mine."

"Like hell we'll take him there. I've got a wife and two cats to watch out for. We'll take him to the zoo."

"What if they don't want him?"

"I'll talk them into it. Do you think we can haul

him into town in an open pickup without his jumping out and killing somebody?"

"He's not dangerous. I'll tie him in so he won't fall out and hurt himself."

"Let's do it then. I don't want anybody coming up this road and seeing what we're doing. The crazy hicks up here are gun-crazy."

"You think somebody might really shoot him?"

"I don't doubt it for a minute. Get him up on his feet and let's head for the zoo. You'll probably have to sit in back with him to keep him calm."

Archie talked the bear into getting into the back of the pickup, then tied the rope around him in a couple of places and tied the ends to the truck's door handles.

"Great, Archie! Now how am I supposed to get into the cab?"

He shrugged — a huge gesture — and untied the rope on the driver's side. I slid in behind the wheel and Archie retied the rope.

"We're going for a little ride, Gus," I heard him say. "Hang on, buddy." He climbed in back with his fluffy friend

We got a lot of looks from the occupants of the vehicles we passed going back to Quartz Quarry, but nobody tried to stop us. I wouldn't have either. Once we got to town, things got a bit dicey. While driving through downtown to reach the zoo over by the college, we got more than our share of action. Some folks just waved and looked for the rest of the parade. A few pedestrians even laughed. Some of them ran for cover.

We were within a mile of the zoo when a police car came out of nowhere and started tailing us, flashing its light, and wailing its siren. I was afraid that if I stopped we'd never make it to the zoo. I heard Archie holler for the cop to shut off his siren, and he did. The cop car rode my bumper for that last mile.

We finally pulled up in front of the big iron gates of the Quartz Quarry Municipal Zoo. It was a weekday, fortunately. Folks were at work. Their kids were at school. There were only a few moms with little kids, and some old folks, wandering around.

However, the visitors in the parking, both leaving and just arriving, started gathering around our truck. Most of them kept their distance. Two cops got out of the cruiser and approached us from either side. I hoped to God I'd know one of them, but they were both strangers. While Archie talked to one cop, I talked to mine.

"Just making a delivery to the zoo, officer," I told my guy. He was a beefy fellow in his forties, short as a giraffe, with nice blue eyes that could have torched holes through cast iron.

"Just making a delivery, huh, bub?" he said, in a voice as mild as any Marine sergeant's "What's the story, pal? What's you doing with a wild bear in your truck?"

"Gus isn't wild," I said. "You can pet him if you want to. He's like a baby. Listen, you remember the newspaper story about Gus, two or three months back?"

"You mean the bear that killed that guy?"

"He was only following orders. It won't happen again. He's sorry. He's pledged to go straight."

"I'm goin' to shoot him."

"You want to shoot a four-hundred-pound bear with a thirty-eight-caliber revolver, be my guest. I'll make sure your wife gets the leftovers. And I don't mean leftover bear."

"I got a shotgun in the squad car."

"You kill that bear and I'll make sure every little kid in this town knows your name and badge number. You'll be Quartz Quarry's biggest heel. I've got a friend who works for the Gladiator. He'll write up a real nice story about you." I glanced in the rearview mirror to see how Archie was managing with his cop. He was saying a lot of polite things, and damned if the flatfoot didn't seem to be listening to him.

"This bear's a danger to the public," my cop said. "You see all these ladies and kids and old folks? I gotta protect 'em."

"Calm down. Quit thinking with your nightstick. Just let me talk to the zoo director."

The truck was rocking back and forth. Gus was restless. He let out a couple of growls, but they sounded half-hearted.

I got lucky. Somebody had already informed the zoo director of our presence. I watched as a little guy waded through the cautious crowd and came up next to my officer. He was wearing a swell sharkskin suit and shiny shoes, and he'd even thought to put on his dove-gray fedora.

"I'm Duncan Freebly, zoo director," he told me and my cop. His voice was a soothing purr. "Is this your bear?"

"He's nobody's at present," I said, "but I hope he's going to be yours. His name is Gus. He's been hibernating out in the mountains, but he came from a circus."

"The bear that killed the man up near Flinder's Cone?'

"Why does everybody keep bringing that up? Gus is quite tame. He'll make an excellent addition to your fine zoo. I'm sure he doesn't eat much. Do you have an empty cage for him?"

The big cop butted in. The other one was working the crowd, trying to keep it from getting closer to the truck.

"I gotta shoot this bear," my cop told Freebly.

"In front of all these children?" Freebly opened his arms and gestured at the collection of moms and toddlers who were gawking at Gus. I liked the guy.

"Well, no," said Big Cop. "I guess we'll have the truck drive someplace more private. But I gotta shoot that bear."

"I know just the place to go," said Freebly. He turned to me. "Drive right through the gates, then turn left on the first road you see. It leads to an alley. Turn right at the alley and — But, here, let me show you. I'll just hop up on your running board if you don't mind." I loved this guy. "We'll just put Gus into a holding cage, and then this fine officer can shoot him. I hope the little children won't be frightened by the gunshots, or the cries of the dying bear." He gave me a secret wink.

I tipped my hat at Officer Big Cop. "Just follow us, please. And don't forget your shotgun."

19

I pulled through the big open gates of the zoo. A road goes through the whole place so folks can drive instead of walk if that suits them. Kind of like a drive-in movie. I pulled into the little side road that bordered the monkey house and found the alley and went up it. Freebly had me drive a little farther and stop in back of what must have been the building that housed the big cats, judging from the sounds that were coming from inside.

"This will have to do," Freebly told me. "We had a tiger die of indigestion recently. His cage is in here. We'll find a place for Gus among our other bears as soon as possible."

I saw in my rearview mirror that the squad car had followed us. It stopped and the big cop got out again. The other boy in blue must have stayed behind to deal with the crowds.

"What is your name, Officer?" Freebly asked, as the big cop came up to us. Freebly was still standing on the running board and still was nowhere near eye-to-eye with the cop.

"Gralmarkey. Sergeant Gralmarkey. Listen, I see what you's trying to do. I ain't come off the last grain boat."

"Why, I'm sure you haven't. But let's be sensible. I have an empty cage where this bear can be kept in safety. It's only a few yards from where we now stand. I'll go get one of my keepers, and Gus can be escorted to his new quarters. You can assist, if you'd like. Once the bear is in its cage it will be a danger to no one. There will be no necessity to shoot it. I'm going to call the police headquarters and explain the situation. Perhaps you'd like to talk to one of your superiors."

"I got a radio in the car, Mr. Freebly. Listen, this bear's stolen goods, as I understand."

"What better place to keep stolen goods than in a cage at the zoo? I'll contact the owners at once. If I can find them."

The truck lurched, and we all looked back. It was Archie jumping down from the truck bed. A moment later he was talking to Freebly.

"Let me put Gus in the cage," he said. "He'll get scared otherwise. He's tame, he really is. I'll show you."

Archie untied Gus's ropes and let down the pickup's tailgate. Gus came out of the truck bed as gentle as a pet calf.

"I can help you find Gus's owner," Archie told Freebly. "The circus Gus worked for ought to be in Yucca Center by now, if they kept to their schedule. I'm the guy that stole Gus. I'm out of jail already. But I can help you get in touch with my old boss."

"Very kind of you," said Freebly. He turned to Officer Gralmarkey. "Is everything arranged to your satisfaction?"

Gralmarkey put one hand on his revolver and the other on his nightstick and shook his head. "I don't know. I got to talk to my captain." Good, he was shifting the responsibility to somebody else. Always a good sign. "I want to see this bear get in its cage first."

"Certainly. It will only take a moment. Allow me to call on one of my keepers."

He went into a side door in the building and came out a couple of minutes later with a blond guy dressed in kaki. I got out of the Studebaker, but nobody needed me. Freebly, Archie, and the blond guy guided Gus into the building. I followed, as did Officer Gralmarkey.

We went down a linoleum-floored hall to a green iron door that looked scarcely big enough to admit Gus, but — with some reluctance — he went through.

"You can go into the main part of the building and say goodbye to your friend," Freebly told Archie. I was beginning to have warm feelings for this zoo director.

We all went through another door, down a hall, and through a second door, and all of a sudden we were surrounded by people and caged cats. And there was Gus, wandering around in a big cage all by himself. I think he a little confused, if I read bear faces correctly. Archie went up to the bars and put his hand through. The big bear came over and nuzzled him. It would have made a nice picture.

"I'm going to make my report now," Gralmarkey growled, trying to look like he was somehow in charge.

"Excellent, Officer," said Freebly. He shook the cop's hand and thanked him for all his assistance.

"Never know what's going to happen in this town," the big cop said. He turned on his heel and left by the main entrance to the cat house.

The zoo director smiled at me. "I'm accustomed to dealing with difficult animals," he told me, and I knew he wasn't talking about Gus.

I decided to bring Archie home with me, feed him sandwiches, let him cry on Tracy's shoulder, and give him a couple of stiff drinks. I had a bottle in the glove box of Tracy's Chevy.

I hadn't heard from Ambrose since our little fight. He was a hard man to deal with. I finally called him. He answered the phone on the first ring. Probably playing checkers with himself.

"Hatfield!"

"Ambrose? This is Axe Hatchett."

"You calling to brag about having fingered Cuthbert for that bear business?"

"No. I just wanted to see how you were doing. If you ever want company, I'm up for a couple of games of checkers. You doing OK by yourself?"

"I like being alone. I got one word for you, Hatchett. Stay away from my sister."

"Sure. Did you hear that the Reaper's in the zoo?"

"Read it in the papers. I might just visit that zoo someday with my rifle in my hands."

"Come on, leave the bear alone. Your brother's dead, and the guy who trained Gus the Reaper is in the can. Get on with your life."

"I'll get on with it. Drop by for checkers some-time. Do you know how to cook?"

"Not so you'd notice. I'll bring sandwiches."

Archie gave me Gus's bullet-proof vest — a creation of Whip Royster's — as a souvenir. The kittens — now cat-sized — sniffed it over and didn't like it at all. They hissed and puffed at it and acted like wild things.

It was too big and smelly to keep as a souvenir of the case, so I cut a strip of fur off of it and hand-ed the rest over to the cops.

Whip Royster got prison time. He also admitted to having been the guy who took a couple of shots at me. That got him a little more time in the ice-box.

When we could, Tracy and I started putting away some money for our deferred honeymoon. She still wanted to go to a dude ranch. She told me she kind of missed the pitter-pat of huge feet in our apartment, but she suggested that our next guest might be a lot smaller.

"No baby yet," I said. "We can't afford it. Concentrate on planning a honeymoon. By the way, what if a bear shows up at the dude ranch and chases us on our cayuses?"

"I've already thought of that. I'm going to buy you an elephant gun for you birthday. And a ten-gallon hat."

"Just buy me a new fedora. I'm getting tired of wearing one with a bullet hole in it."

END

If you have enjoyed this book, please go to its Amazon book page and leave a short review. It will be most appreciated!

OTHER BOOKS BY THIS AUTHOR:

DEAD MAN LIMPING
[ISBN: 978-1-940469-00-3]

When 1950s private eye Axel Hatchett is hired by a delectable redhead to turn up her missing husband, Hatchett discovers that the man is not only still alive, but is armed, probably crazy, and is on a killing spree that may include Hatchett! But something stinks about this case — big time — and it's not Hatchett's pet skunk, Ambrosia.

GLIMMER IN A GLASS EYE
[ISBN: 978-1-940469-02-7]

After 1950s gumshoe Axel Hatchett is hired to protect a used car dealer from a threat of murder, Hatchett finds himself in a nest of rattlesnakes — literally! When the car dealer is bumped off, and Hatchett's prime suspect is murdered, the sleuth is forced to sift through a deck of also-ran suspects to solve the two killings before another corpse is added. And to make matters worse, he's falling for a mouthy waitress who works in a sleazy diner....

SLAYER IN A GRAY TOUPEE
[ISBN: 978-1-940469-01-0]

Rumpled 1950s sleuth, Axel Hatchett, is summoned to the Flinders Mansion to prevent a millionaire's threatened murder. After a fierce blizzard knocks out the power and closes the roads, Hatchett is trapped in the candle-lit mansion with an eccentric array of terrified guests and servants. The detective is determined to solve the case, but his only clue is a sinister gray toupee.

THREE CURSING BIRDS
[ISBN: 978-1-940469-03-4]

When thieves snatch a statue of the bird-headed Egyptian god, Thoth, and drop its owner from a third-story window, 1950s private detective Axel Hatchett is set on their trail. But wait! – there are actually three statues, and one of them may contain a treasure map! Hatchett enlists the aid of his hash-slinging fiancée and a snake-handling English professor to help solve the case of the three cursed birds.

BOOK CLUB DISCUSSION QUESTIONS
(To Be Discussed With Whiskey And A Hearty Squirrel Stew)

1. How did you experience this book? Did you feel amused, sad...dyspeptic?

2. Describe the main characters — their personality traits, motivations, inner qualities (or lack thereof).

3. What was Cuthbert's motivation? What about the motivations for Ambrose, Archie, and Whip? What about for Custer the cattle dog? (oops! — he's in the next one...)

4. What main ideas does the author explore? The same old tropes about love, treachery, greed, and the pettiness of humanity? (it's a hard boiled mystery, for crying out loud!)

5. To the main point — did it make you laugh? Why?

6. Was the ending satisfying? If so, why? If not, why not? Should Gus have eaten Axel? You do realize he's the main character, right? (Axe, not Gus)

7. Describe the dynamics between the members of the Hatfield family. No snickering.

8. How has the past changed the lives of the characters? — both the Hatfields and Gus.

9. How have the main characters changed over the course of the five books? Who has changed the most? Who has changed the least? Who do you hope to see murdered in the next book?

10. Would you buy another novel by this author? You're on the fifth book, so this has obviously become a habit.

ABOUT THE AUTHOR

Steven LeRoy Nelson is an award-winning humorist whose short fiction has appeared in *Alfred Hitchcock Mystery Magazine, Ellery Queen Mystery Magazine, The Leviathan,* and numerous other publications.

Visit him at his website at:

www.stevenleroynelson.com